OBSESSIONS

OBSESSIONS

CESAR J. ROTONDI

St. Martin's Press
New York

Library of Congress Cataloging in Publication Data

Rotondi, Cesar J
    Obsessions.

    I. Title.
PZ4.R84920b [PS3568.0878] 813'.5'4 79-22863
ISBN 0-312-58052-5

Table of Contents

OBSESSIONS

TATU

I'm so glad to meet someone who's really interested. I could tell you had exceptional taste the minute I saw you. Why don't we sit at a table and I'll tell you the whole story. But let me have a schnapps this time. Beer runs through an old woman so fast, and I don't want to get up every ten minutes. You wouldn't believe how filthy they let the toilets get in this hole. In the old days they'd have been fined.

"That's better. Let me start by telling you about Rudi. He was very young when he got started, but right from the beginning he was one of the cleverest artists in the business. He opened his first shop in Hamburg, the perfect place to get a small tattoo parlor going. A little rough maybe, but tattooists have to have a sailor town unless they become so specialized or famous that they can set up somewhere else.

"No, there weren't many with Rudi's talent and hardly any with his imagination. He was clean, too, and he never hurt, even when he was working on very sensitive areas, and he sure worked on some; but I don't want to get ahead of my story.

"Rudi himself was tattooed in the Japanese style. Do you know what that means? There aren't too many examples around any more. In the Japanese style the background of the design is all filled in with black or dark blue so the design is formed in reverse, you see? Western

4

tattoos are drawn right on the skin. One is positive, one negative.

"Rudi ran away to sea when he was only fourteen, and he sailed the China Seas until he quit. He must have started getting tattooed in one of the Oriental ports when he was still a kid because it takes years to finish a job like that. Wasn't there a picture of the Japanese style in the postcards you were looking at today? There are some, usually, but as I say there are fewer and fewer examples around. Rudi's entire body was covered up to his wrist and ankle and collar line so that when he was fully dressed you would never know, but naked he was just one great piece of dark patchwork. I tell you, it was really spooky the first time I saw him, but fascinating too. I think I still prefer natural flesh tones around the design, but the experts all say the Japanese is more artistic.

"You've got to be pretty interested in tattooing to get yourself all done up that way, and since Rudi was so creative it wasn't long before he tried his own hand at it. While he was still on ship he started working on some of the men sailing with him, and it was clear right from the start that he had natural talent. He was barely twenty when he gave up sailing and decided to give all his time to tattoo.

"God knows where Rudi came from; I don't think he was ever sure himself, but he knew Hamburg and liked it. He found a tiny place near the harbor with a room in back to live in and hung out a sign. He was pretty much a loner and was happy to spend all his time there except for an occasional trip to St. Pauli to get laid. The Reeperbahn wasn't really his style, but he liked to get things over with quickly without getting too involved.

"It was in one of those dives in St. Pauli that he met Magda. She was a good little girl, honest and straight from the farm, but you know how things were then. It was about 1930 or '31, and a poor girl would hump her heart out for a ham sandwich. She must have been damn happy to get off the streets and move into that one small room behind the shop. Yes, just one room. But it had a stove and toilet right in it and Rudi wasn't bad. Ugly as a monkey even without the tattoos, but not a bad man.

"I guess what he liked most about Magda was that she didn't talk much. She was plain and clean and she was there when he wanted her, and that was enough for him.

"It was just natural for him to start tattooing Magda. He'd have tattooed the furniture if he could when the shop wasn't busy. I don't think she was interested, really, but it wouldn't have been like her to refuse anything he suggested. He started with some simple, pretty things at first. A flower on her ass, and then a butterfly on the other cheek to balance it. I've never known a man to love his work as much as Rudi. When he couldn't do it on a customer he'd do it as a hobby. As soon as the shop closed he'd open a beer and go to work on Magda, the way some men will take out a stamp collection when they get home or watch the football game.

"It wasn't long before Magda's back was covered with a copy of Venus he took from some Italian painter, with one hand up to her tit, and coming out of the water with her hair all blowy. Even before that was finished, though, her ass and legs were already one big collection of flowers, butterflies, and sea shells. Very pretty.

"By now Rudi was starting to make a name for himself. And tattooing was very much in style then. You should have seen the King of Denmark—King Frederick, it was. He loved to pose with his shirt off, just the same as any other sailor. Jesus, he was a good-looking man. And some very refined English ladies, too. Always looking for something artistic.

"As you can imagine, word got out about Rudi's own body, and a lot of his customers used to ask him to strip before he went to work on them. But Rudi was very modest. There were some tattoo artists who had some interesting work on them who used to work in shorts, but not Rudi. He always had on a white coat and sailor pants. Oh sure, he'd strip down without a word as soon as he was asked. But after they'd had a look he'd put his clothes right on again and wash his hands before going to work. He was always washing his hands, Rudi. So clean.

"Pretty soon the word got out how good he was and customers with more unusual tastes started coming around. He began to make a lot more money. You can charge anything you want to a customer who's looking for something really special, but Rudi never went overboard. As a matter of fact, if a young sailor wanted something done that Rudi thought was a little too offbeat he'd send him away for a couple of days to let the kid be sure he really wanted it before he'd start. Oh, Rudi had ethics. And if they were nice kids he'd never charge them more for a special job than he would for the usual roses or panthers or mementoes of mothers and first lays. Oh dear, when you think of it, most of the tattoos people decide on are so boring. What a burden they must be. Imagine showing your children your forearm with 'To Mary—Till Death Do Us Part,' when their mother's name is Anna. But never mind. I'd love another schnapps, okay? Thanks.

"As far as I know, there were only two other tattooists working in those days, or ever since, who had what you could call really great style. There was a Dr. Sparrow in London whose specialty was tattooing a fly on the head of a prick. I tell you they were so realistic you wanted to swat them. And there was a strange man in Chicago who they said was Rasputin's assistant. Dr. Basil specialized in *The Last Supper*. There must be fifty people still wandering around with *The Last Supper* across their backs. Of course, Dr. Basil did some other things too, including some pretty bizarre ones. They say he made a lot of money during World War II tattooing sailors' asses with a simple blue seal that said 'U.S. Gov't. Inspected Choice.' I don't get it, but they paid for it.

"The last I heard of Sparrow or Basil they were both still working, but in other cities. It's been years now; I wonder if they're alive.

"Let me get back to Rudi. I think he was the best. I mean, if you have any talent at all you can always depend on your customers' imaginations to come up with something surprising. But Rudi was much more than an artist. He had heart. How many tattooists do you think tell these silly kids that want to get done how expensive and painful it is to have a tattoo removed? Rudi always told them. It's a mess and there's danger of scarring. That's why Rudi was always so careful they knew what they were getting into. He'd never work on anyone he thought had been drinking too much, for example—and let me tell you, half the people who decide to get their first tattoo are loaded when they do it.

"In all those years Rudi never had a case of blood poisoning or even had anyone get really mad at him. You must understand there are always some people who are disappointed when the work is finished. They expect— God knows what. It's like all those crazy people who keep going to plastic surgeons to change their noses and their tits. They want to be loved or to be irresistible. It's too much to ask. But on the other hand, there are always some people who might just get very excited about you if you have the right tattoo in the right place.

"So, that's how Rudi got started. People love to show their tattoos, of course, so if you're any good at all you can start to build a reputation fast. Then there was a vogue for photographing tattooed bodies, and Rudi's body was being photographed regularly. So was Magda's. They got a commission, you know, on postcard sales or reproductions sometimes. Not much, but it was steady. Most of the tattoo parlors had a side business selling the postcards. They used to cost a couple of pennies in those days, ten if they were autographed, and sometimes more if they showed a tattooed dick. Now I'll bet you paid plenty for the ones you bought today, didn't you? Oh yes, they're real collector's items. If I'd known years ago what they'd be getting, I'd be rich today. Well, that's how it goes.

"It was only natural that some customers would start asking for a look at Magda's body, and Rudi didn't hesitate to oblige them. Magda would come out from the back where she'd been listening to the radio—she was always a lazy slut—and then she'd strip down to a G-string and give them a look. The customers always left a tip, and sometimes the tips were large enough to let her know they had something more on their minds than a look.

"Rudi knew when a customer was excited, but it didn't seem important to him at first. Lots of men get a hard-on the minute you start to tattoo them, and he was used to the freaks who would get turned on when he stripped down for them. He'd have guys begging him to let them touch it, or 'examine the designs,' as they used to put it. He'd just put his clothes on before they tried going any further. It's all part of the business. When they got excited around Magda the only way they dared show their interest was by tipping. Rudi was built pretty solid, and you couldn't make anything out behind that straight, hard expression of his, so the customers generally behaved.

"After the money got better, they moved to a new place in the same neighborhood with a nice three-room apartment behind the shop. It was a big move for them and I don't think either one of them had ever known anything as grand.

"As I understand it, it was Magda's idea to start making a little extra money. There was one john who left bigger and bigger tips every time he came around for a look at her. When she told Rudi she was interested in turning a trick he didn't say much one way or the other. I guess he knew it was coming.

"Ten minutes after the john was alone with her the job was over and she'd made enough to pay the rent for a month. Jesus, it was easy. There was no trouble telling when a guy had the hots for her, and Magda found she could charge three times as much as the best-looking whores in St. Pauli and get it. After only two weeks you could see she was going to be bringing in more money than the tattooing. And Rudi was no fool. When he saw the kind of money these johns were ready to part with, he began to let a couple of the interested ones swing on him, although he claimed he never enjoyed it. Hell, if whores had to worry about whether or not they liked it, there'd be a lot fewer people getting laid. They liked the money and they were busy all the time now.

"Rudi never stopped tattooing, of course. Apart from the fact that it gave a special touch to the other business, it was still his first passion and he kept getting better at it. Then, not only was his art being recognized but also people knew he was discreet, so he started getting more men and women coming in for cock or tit tattoos, and then they started coming around too to have their tits pierced so a gold ring or a wooden plug could be passed through. Like I said, Rudi was clean and people trusted him.

"Along about this time Annaliese came around. She had just started as a hooker a short time before and she wandered in because one of her johns said he'd pay her double if she got herself a little tattoo someplace special just for him.

"I tell you, Rudi was used to lots of good-looking women, but he really fell for Annaliese the minute he saw her. She was a little bit of a blonde thing from the south, Partenkirchen I believe, with big Bavarian eyes and tits to match. She must have liked Rudi too, because they humped right there on the tattoo table—something he never did before, except for money of course.

"Rudi asked Annaliese to spend the night because he wanted a little time to decide on exactly the right tattoo for her, and of course she was a great lay. It's hard to believe, but she and Magda liked each other too, right from the start. Not a touch of jealousy. In a couple of days she had moved in with them and Rudi went to work on what many experts feel was his masterpiece.

"A few months later the job was finished. Annaliese had a crucified Christ perfectly tattooed across her body. The nails in the palms went right into her nipples and the nail in the feet went into her navel while the bottom of the cross came to rest right on top of her box. Oh, but the expression on Jesus' face. I tell you, you've never seen anything more beautiful.

"I get awfully dry talking so much. Do you mind if I have another schnapps? Better make it a double; I have a lot more to tell. Ah, you're a real sport. I could always tell the live ones from the stiffs.

"So! The first thing Rudi did when Annaliese was ready was to get in touch with one of Magda's richest tricks and offer him the first go. Oh, Rudi was smart all right. He didn't even let anyone get a peek at her until the work was finished. He had real class.

"Annaliese was a beauty even before she was decorated, and the poor trick nearly creamed the minute he saw her. Rudi took one look at the sucker's face and knew they were going to be rich. He started to make big plans.

"Three months later Rudi was ready to move the shop and the two girls here to Berlin. No question, Berlin was the place to see the money really roll in. There was no taste that couldn't be catered to here, and they'd pay anything for it. Not just Berliners, but rich johns from all over the world came here. I never understood where people got the idea Paris was a good whore's town. Any good Berlin whore *forgot* more about fancy fucking than a Parisian could ever learn. It must have been Berlin's biggest industry. Sure, the competition was stiff, but so were the customers. Ha, excuse me; that one is as old as the profession.

"I told you Rudi was smart. He knew enough to keep the shop very simple. At first Annaliese wanted to put on a white coat too, like a nurse, and be his assistant, but he wouldn't hear of it. She was always more ambitious than that lazy slut Magda. The shop was a little larger, but the only new touch in it were two small photos of the girls, discreetly placed where they could be seen by the clients while he worked. Apart from that, it was just like a doctor's office.

"Although the shop was simple, the house behind the shop sure wasn't. It was as tasteful and elegant as any whorehouse in Berlin. The girls worked in rooms with thick carpets, and all the walls were decorated with photographs of exotically tattooed bodies. They had red silk sheets on the beds and whips and chains and bonds of all sorts for customers who wanted them. By now they had a pretty good idea of where their customers' tastes lay and they were ready to offer highly specialized services.

"The girls had fabulous wardrobes, too, mostly leather of course, and it was Annaliese who made every stitch. She was still basically a little Bavarian *hausfrau* who liked working at things like that.

"Rudi still turned a trick, too, when it was worth his while. He had an English lady, very aristocratic, who paid plenty to take a nap there and then have Rudi come in naked with a hangman's mask over his head to wake her. Nothing else.

"Yes, the customers paid, but they got their money's worth. I guess it was a happy little household they had. No jealousy, plenty of money, and they liked each other.

"After they'd been established a while, a pretty little Berliner named Lulu came by the shop with her boyfriend Peter and started getting friendly. Lulu had shiny black bobbed hair like Lia de Putti and a big, creamy body with hard, boyish tits. Don't know Lia de Putti? Yes, I guess she's been dead a long time. The most beautiful actress in Berlin. She killed herself by eating a box of kitchen matches. Her nymphomania upset her. But you shouldn't let me wander like that. I was telling you about Lulu and Peter. They seemed just like any other couple of young kids in love, except that they were a lot crazier. Peter was a big roughneck type with hands that could hammer nails. When they first came in, he wanted a small heart tattooed on his butt with her name in it. Real corny. Then she got the idea of having a spurt of flame that looked like it was coming out of her ass and going up her back. It turned out very well and they were both pleased.

"A month or so later they came in and said they were getting married and wanted a double-ring ceremony. So Rudi pierced their tits and opened the wedding rings and got them in place. You couldn't properly solder the rings closed, of course, but Lulu wanted to try it. She thought Rudi could put them to sleep with ether or something, but he convinced her that even so there was danger of scarring.

"They were so happy with their rings, and by now they had gotten real chummy with Magda and Annaliese and they'd all have coffee together nearly every afternoon. Rudi said he'd never seen a couple as much in love as they were, but every once in a while she'd show up with a black eye or a bruised jaw, and he always had scratches on his face. Nobody's business but theirs, of course. They were both a little crazy, but Peter had this one side of him—anyway, he got himself mixed up with the Brown Shirts. Don't look that way. Lots of people were, even if they don't talk about it any more. All right, I didn't like it either, but that's the type he was. A real hothead, and the Party knew how to use bruisers like him in those brawls; *provocations* I think they call them today. Peter never knew his own strength. He ended up murdering someone, an old Jew it was, who couldn't have stood up to anyone half Peter's size. Peter might have been able to get away with it a few years later, but this was only 1932 or so and there were still a lot of people in Germany who didn't see which way the wind was blowing.

"He got a life sentence, but he managed to have a little time off before they sentenced him to put his affairs in order. The day before he was to go to prison he took Lulu to Rudi. If you don't mind, I could really use another double schnapps. This part of the story upsets me. Maybe you'd better have one too.

"Rudi had heard some pretty strange requests from clients, and by now he usually enjoyed doing them, but this was one job he absolutely refused—at first. They won out in the end because they got him excited about it, and Rudi couldn't turn down a new challenge if he believed it was something the customer really wanted.

"First, Peter had his foreskin pierced at the tip and then a small gold lock passed through it. It's not a particularly painful operation, but it's rough getting a hard-on after that even if you don't intend to do anything with it. Peeing's no problem, but other things must be. You've never heard of piercing foreskins? Well, sealing them off that way is probably unusual today, but a hundred years ago it was done to young boys all the time to keep them from playing with themselves. Infibulation, they call it. When I was a young girl I saw plenty of dicks that still had holes in the foreskin; Germans, Englishmen. Thank God they don't worry about things like that any more, but during the last war a ring in the foreskin was still fairly popular, especially with sailors in submarine service. They were all a strange lot anyway.

"Maybe you'd better drink up too. After the lock was in place, Lulu had the key put in her cunt and the lips sewn up. I'm sorry, drink some water. That's called infibulation too, and it's not all that rare. They still do it to young girls or babies in many parts of the world. I told you Lulu was a little crazy. If she ever changed her mind she could always be opened up again. And he could always have the lock snapped. Personally, I wouldn't do it for a million marks, but to them it was the final act of love, and when you come right down to it, it's no sillier than killing yourselves, which some lovers have been known to do.

"I didn't *say* it was going to be a pretty story. Anyway, after Peter was sent away Lulu kept coming around, and she was always crying that she was sure she'd never hear from him again. I think she was just seventeen. God, how young.

"As it turned out, she never did hear from him again.

Maybe he figured it was better that way or maybe somebody did him in, but nobody ever found out what happened to Peter or whether he left his little gold lock on.

"Lulu started to really go nuts, and pretty soon she asked Rudi to let her work in the house. She'd never turned a trick before but she was dead serious. Does that really sound so strange to you? Maybe, but for a lot of girls who go to work in whorehouses it's like giving up sex. Or are you one of those people who wonder if whores have orgasms? Well, I'll tell you—some do. Just some. But for a lot of pros it's just a job, only you use your pussy instead of your back. Don't worry about it.

"Rudi was aware, naturally, that a lot of his customers with more exotic tastes would be really turned on by the idea of a sewed-up box, and Lulu convinced him that it wasn't going to stop her from giving them a good time. He probably had the hots for her himself by this time, so after she gave him the first sample of what she could do, he ran right to the telephone to call in one of his kinkiest johns.

"They loved her. In no time at all she was being hailed as the best cocksucker in Berlin, and even Rudi hardly bothered with the other girls any more. At least for a while.

"Personally, I don't think she could have been that great except for two things. First, her tricks were already very turned on by her pussy. She was eaten half to death by most of her johns. You can't imagine how excited some men get by that sort of thing. Maybe they thought she was a virgin. But secondly—and most important, I think—when she lived with Peter they used to play very rough. I guess they both must have liked it. Anyway, over the year or so they were together he had managed to knock most of her teeth out and loosen the rest. Lulu wore a beautiful set of plates that looked absolutely real. Hell, you just didn't think of a pretty young girl like that with false teeth. Well, when she started to work on a john she'd give a little cough and sneak out her teeth and stuff them under the mattress. I doubt that her johns ever got wise but they probably wouldn't have cared much if they did. It was easy for her and they probably never had a better blow job.

"Ah yes, those were the days, my friend. Rudi's House of Tatu became internationally famous. Two new girls started—I'm not sure where he found them. Lots of girls used to come around asking to be tattooed so they could work there, but it wasn't worth the effort to do all that work on just any old whore.

"The first of the two new girls was a tall black from the Ivory Coast named Sara—and I mean real tall. Her face and body were completely covered with arrow-shaped scars that were blue-black. In her part of the world they start on you when you're a child and just carve in with a knife and then rub the pigment into the wound. Yes, that's the way they tattoo. And black skin has a funny way of scarring that's different from ours—thick welts. She also had her teeth filed to sharp points. Not much future there as a cocksucker, but all you had to do was put her in a pair of boots and shove a whip in her hand and there'd be a file of English lords halfway down the street. Even Rudi admitted she was ugly as the devil, but what the hell, you can't argue with customers.

"Then there was a petite redhead named Eva who was tattooed in the Japanese style, just like Rudi, except that her tattoos covered everything—face, hands, and feet too, even the soles. Her hair was exceptionally striking against all that dark skin, I must say, and she was very proud of it. Not that the poor dear didn't have her problems. When she went out she'd plaster her face with clown white and powder it all down, and then top the whole thing off with a mourning veil. A lot of trouble, but she stayed in most of the time anyway and we all liked her. She had a really sweet disposition and was the best cook in the house. Indonesian cooking.

"Then one day Rudi heard about the American Fucking

Machine. No, not really a machine; let me tell you. But first how about another double schnapps.

"Berlin had never had so many fancy whorehouses as at this time, and there must have been a few even more famous than the House of Tatu. Word started to get around about a really fantastic one-woman house operated by a group of SS men. God only knows where they found this poor creature; she must have had a pathetic life. Anyway, however they got her, once they saw what she could do they took a small apartment just outside an army barracks at the edge of the city. Cheap rent, and they were soon making a fortune on her. The poor thing was deaf and dumb and not very bright, and she weighed nearly 400 pounds. All it took was a room with a strong bed, someone to stand outside and take in money, and a bushel of sugar cane next to the bed. Yes, sugar cane. She was fed normal meals three times a day, but she would munch on these great chunks of sugar cane all the time she worked. And I mean she worked. The poor dear never got off her back. Those big legs would grip a man around the hips and toss him up like a toy. I've heard of technique before, but they say no man could last more than ten minutes with her and most of them a lot less. The turnover was incredible. And the reason they called her the *American* Fucking Machine was that she had an American flag tattooed on her arm when they found her. Nothing else. If she had a name she didn't know it and no one ever bothered to find out.

"You can bet the SS men would have held on to her forever if they could, but with an attraction like that it's hard to go unnoticed. Word reached SS headquarters and they realized they'd have to get rid of her fast. They came to Rudi first. Maybe they thought he'd be interested because of her tattoo. Rudi thought about it for a while, talked it over with the other girls, and finally decided to buy her. They never told me the exact price, but I know the American Fucking Machine cost the House of Tatu a full six months' income.

"The girls tried making friends with her but there wasn't much point. All she knew was eating and fucking, both in volume. Did you ever try to eat sugar cane? I tried once and my jaws got tired. Boring and highly indigestible; all those tough fibers. She actually chewed and swallowed the whole thing.

"There was no point trying to change her screwing technique or teach her some new tricks. Maybe it was because she wouldn't put that sugar cane down even for a minute. But it didn't matter. She was a master at her own style. The minute a man got near her, those legs would whip out and grab him like a vise, all the while she munched the cane, and from then on he didn't have much choice. Munch, crunch, munch, crunch. Boom.

"What a challenge for Rudi. As I said, he was a true artist, and now here was the biggest canvas he'd ever seen laid out before him. Like a portrait painter facing his first cathedral ceiling. I hate to think how many bushels of sugar cane she must have gone through before it was finished, but when it was all over she was decorated with more American flags and eagles and even some American Indians plus lifelike portraits of all the presidents of the United States right up to Franklin Roosevelt. Nice, heh? Rudi would never have tried a theme that wasn't related to the tattoo she already had.

"At first Rudi thought he'd charge more for her because she was pretty special, but then he decided to put a bargain price on her since she could really do it wholesale. She was certainly something to see, but very few people ever saw more than the front, and then not for very long. What a money maker! Rudi says he never screwed her— not his style—but I think she had a crush on him. You got the feeling no one had ever been so nice to her. She loved Eva's cooking, too, and the sugar cane never stopped. She actually put on more weight. Yes, some.

"I was the last to join them. Just let me unbutton my blouse a little and if you'll lean over this way I'll show you. There! My real name is Gaby, but I was known as

Serpentina. You can just see two of the heads here, the cobra and the python, but there are actually five snakes winding around my torso and my arms and legs, all accurate down to the last scale. Nothing quite as far out as some of the others, but I had my fans, and you must admit these are very artistically done. I suppose we were photographed almost as much as any movie star. There were postcards with our pictures on them all over the world. Except for Lulu's pictures, of course. There were plenty of her too, but they were much more expensive, like the ones of Rudi's dick, and only for the richest private collections.

"You'd think there'd be no end to all the money that was pouring in, but something always comes along to screw things up. In this case it was Eva, the one with the Japanese tattoos. Not her fault—we were all careful about screening customers—but one of her tricks got a bit too carried away. How can you tell what a man's going to do if he's excited enough? God knows she was used to all sorts of rough handling; a lot of it faked, of course, but plenty of it for real too. Anyway, there she was one night with her neck broken and the place full of johns and all hell breaking loose. Ordinarily, those things can be taken care of. Rudi spent a fortune trying to set things right and we thought everything was going to be fine. It would have been, too, except for one son of a bitch of an officer who was in the place that night—one of Lulu's tricks, as I recall. He was a mean bastard and he was out to get Rudi. And Eva's accident was just an excuse.

"You see, Rudi was a Rom, a full-blooded gypsy, and this officer was one of those fanatics who believed all that race crap of Hitler's. Believe me, the war would have ended very differently if it weren't for all that crazy business. Perhaps you don't know it, but there was a higher percentage of gypsies that ended in the camps than Jews. You don't hear about it as much because there were quite a few Jews who either bought their way out or managed to escape during the early years. And later, you know, Jews all read and write and they have a lot of their own to tell what happened to them. But gypsies are an illiterate bunch, and let's face it, there are plenty of people even today who wouldn't shed a tear if they never saw another gypsy. They've never been too popular anywhere, I suppose.

"Rudi would have bought his way out if he'd any idea what was coming, but it never occurred to him. I don't think anyone knew what was really going on. The son of a bitch officer came and took Rudi away himself.

"Once Rudi was gone, Magda tried running the house, but it didn't work. There were plenty of customers, all right, but there was no organization and we were always having trouble. I hate to admit it, but a whore doesn't have a chance if there's not a man around.

"Then the war got worse, and by now everyone was starting to suffer, not just the whores. The military took over everything. A soldier's needs came first and of course that included women. Magda and I got sent to a government whorehouse near the front lines. They used us as a piece of meat for about six months—I don't think we could have lasted a year. After that it was the work camps. Twelve hours a day working in those lousy slave factories. Some Jews worked there too. Just a matter of trying to get as much out of you as possible before you croaked.

"Later I was told they shot Sara, and Lulu killed herself, never mind how. The American Fucking Machine? They sent her to one of their hospitals. That's a hell of a word for them, isn't it? What do you suppose they could do with a 400-pound deaf and dumb halfwit whose body was a course in American history? Better not to think about it. We already know too much about those bastards. As you can see, I got through, and I hope Magda did too, but she was pretty sick the last time I saw her.

"I ended up in East Berlin after the Armistice, not far from where the old House of Tatu used to be, working in a nursing home where the soup pots smelled as bad as the piss pots. But I got out and came to the west. It's easier than you think if you're an old woman and just another mouth for the state to feed. Ha! I walked right out and they let me. Of course they let me; don't believe everything you read.

"Life is funny, isn't it? Well here I am, still strong and healthy in spite of all I went through, and a lot smarter too. And now I have a surprise. Rudi is alive. Yes. The Russians took him from his camp and he was brought to Russia for rehabilitation. Just another damn labor camp, of course, but now he knew at least that he could survive. And he did. He made it to Berlin three years ago, on foot most of the way, and he found me the same way you did, through Alex, the man in the bookstore who still sells some of the old pictures. I took him right in, you can be sure.

"Listen to me, all we need is a little money to get started again. Not very much. You'd be a partner; that goes without saying. The bookseller told me you spent almost a hundred marks on those pictures. I tell you, it wouldn't take more than a few thousand at first. We know all the ropes. Rudi is still a great artist. Sure, he could never have handled a needle when he first got back, but he's all rested now and he's dying to get back to work. Look, he's not even seventy yet and he's strong— strong as a bull, I tell you. You can't kill those old gypsies.

"I'm not looking for a handout. I want a partner.

"We can make a fortune again, *a fortune*. I know times change and tastes change, but they change back again, too. Can you deny that the time is right? Now, right *now*. I can feel it. It would work in London or New York or Amsterdam or anywhere. *The streets are full of whores* and there's never been a better market for what we have to offer. What do you say, eh? Can you think of a better time for it than now?"

VATICAN
CONTESSA

Not the number tens! It's morning, you goose. My number six pearls, the triple."

Olga's voice was reedy but offered no hint of temper, either suppressed or restrained. Her eyes looked straight ahead into the triple mirror of the dressing table while her head rotated slowly from one side to the other, scanning her reflection as methodically as a radar receiver.

Meli stood behind her, dangling the pearls over her like a garrote, until a nod signaled her to lower them and fasten the clasp. Meli was slight as a sparrow and as nervous.

"There we are, Contessa. You must excuse me, but I'm not thinking straight today. It's my head again. I'm having a terrible morning—it happens when it's time for my period." The last words were barely whispered and she pursed her lips over them.

"You haven't had a period in nearly twenty years." Olga's expressionless eyes never left the mirror as a gloved hand reached up to finger a pearl and then pat the necklace reassuringly.

"I didn't say I was having a period. I mean—" she stammered, "it's when it would have been my time. I feel them just the same. Nausea, headache, and my feet hurt more than usual." She bit her upper lip and winced.

"Do you still drink red wine?"

"Oh no, Contessa. You know I don't drink. Only at breakfast. A little glass with a biscuit. It holds me all morning."

"Don't. Take one glass of camomile in the morning, then two glasses of white wine and two glasses of mineral water—Sangemini is best—with your meals and just before retiring. You'll lose your pains." Olga lifted her chin and caressed the skin of her throat with her gloved hand.

"But Contessa, two glasses of white wine would make me—"

"Enough." Olga fluttered her hand impatiently. "You're as strong as a horse. There isn't anyone in your whole family who doesn't live to be a hundred. Now, about this morning. The viewing will be in the shade, but then we'll probably be moving about a bit at the reception afterward and I expect there will be sun. Do you think I should wear the black straw with the wide brim?"

"There's no sun this morning, Contessa. It's like lead out."

"Go and look again. If you don't think the sun might come out, bring me the black and white with the little daisies."

She widened her eyes and ran a finger gingerly across the skin beneath them. It seemed only faintly puffy, and the color had been bleached to the palest lilac. She sniffed appreciatively at her cosmetic skill. Next, she forced her mouth into a wide grimace, pushing her lips as widely as possible into a leering rictus, and then tensed and released her jaw muscles repeatedly to exercise them. She had trained herself not to smile too broadly in public, because if she did—or if she allowed her speech to become too animated—it was quickly apparent that the flesh around her mouth remained unresponsive, the nerve endings there quite deadened after her fifth surgical adjustment. It had taken long, disciplined practice, but now she could speak with her lips only slightly parted, and by raising and lowering her voice a little more than was natural, she could give the effect of unimpeded speech.

Olga fingered the small pearl in a chased gold setting at her left ear and then allowed her finger to move back and graze the wealed skin a few centimeters behind the lobe. Her face tensed, and she scanned it again, section by section, searching for a new unnoticed blemish or the intrusion of an unfamiliar thread on the waxy surface.

"Cruel," she thought, "to hold these affairs in the morning, and outside as well. This one shall be my last."

"Here you are, Contessa." Meli was holding the black and white hat dotted with daisies.

"No, better bring me the straw. After the Swiss Guards I'm going to Lawyer Gorizia to interview his new protegée, and he'll probably insist on having lunch on the terrace."

"But it's very cloudy. And anyway, wouldn't he have the table set up in the shade?" Meli thrust the hat at her encouragingly.

"Don't argue. What's wrong with you this morning? Don't you know sunlight can come through clouds and even burn you if you're outside long enough? The straw."

Olga Seppi-Gianotti rose from her dressing table and crossed the room, trying not to look at the unmade bed with half a dozen small lacy pillows scattered across its head. She hated untidiness and wished there were a separate dressing room like the one she had had at the villa in Nebbia. There, even her bathroom had a couch and makeup table and a little secretary for finishing up correspondence. Then she remembered all too readily the years in Nebbia when they had been without running water for days on end. She sighed.

The apartment she now occupied in Prati was, after all, quite comfortable by most standards. She used the largest room as her bedroom, remembering her mother's reminder that it was foolish not to use the most spacious room for the one you were in most. And like her mother, she rarely received in her salon, preferring, without apology, to lead the few intimates who called directly to her bedroom.

At Nebbia all the reception rooms and dining areas were on the ground floor, but her mother had converted a whole upstairs wing for her private apartment. When Olga eventually inherited the villa, her life had already been well established in Rome. But she thought of the villa often and the inevitable comparisons were usually colored by nostalgia.

She moved to a wooden wardrobe, heavy with carved cherubs wreathed in garlands. It had stood once in Nebbia and was too large for the wall it now filled. She opened one of the doors, and the full-length mirror behind it caught the reflection of the unmade bed and the cluttered vanity table. She frowned and swung the door until they were out of view and then straightened stiffly before it.

Her figure was quite good. She smoothed the waist of her dress and swung her hips sharply to allow the skirt to make a decisive swish and then settle into fresh folds. The seams of her stockings appeared straight, and she wondered again how very few people could possibly notice that she wore only real silk. Her calves were shapely and her ankles—well, perhaps a shade too thin, but still! Her feet were small and had been crammed into even smaller pumps with precariously high heels.

I doubt that we'll be standing much, she speculated, *except after the investiture. But I can probably break away from that after only—*

A sharp twinge caught her in the small of the back and spread painfully down her right thigh. She caught her breath and steadied herself against the closet for a moment, then opened another door and took out a pair of black sandals with a conservative heel. She gritted her teeth and sat on the divan to change her shoes. "Meli!"

"I can't find the black straw in the hall closet."

"I know, I know. I put it back in here last week. Come and help me with my shoes. I can't bend."

Meli shuffled in, not even slightly disgruntled, and knelt to pry off a shoe. "Oh dear, your feet are all red. You should throw those silly shoes away. They don't fit you at all."

Olga tossed her head. "It's just because you didn't rub them yesterday. As soon as I get back from lunch you can give them a good rub, first alcohol, and then that new cream. When my feet have been cared for properly I can dance all night in those shoes."

Meli arched an eyebrow but said nothing.

"There. They're perfectly hideous, but I suppose for this hour of the day they'll be all right." She stood again and looked into the mirror, drawing herself up as tall as she could so that she was now fully a head taller than Meli, who seemed to be looking at her approvingly.

"Am I all right?"

"Perfect, Contessa."

"The hat's in there," she gestured.

She took it delicately from Meli and fitted it on carefully, then checked for any wisps of hair that might have strayed.

"How do I look?"

"Perfect, Contessa."

"Will you please stop saying that. You sound stupid. Try to be objective when someone asks you a question. Do you think he got my hair too blonde yesterday?" She turned to give Meli a better look at her hair, which hung loosely in a smooth sheet just to her shoulder.

"To tell the truth, I liked it better when you wore it in two buns. Or when you piled it all on your head, like the night you went to—"

Olga turned to her testily. "For God's sake, Meli. That was—I was a girl then."

"No, you weren't." Meli reddened for fear of having been too outspoken.

Olga softened and patted Meli's arm. "You're quite right, my dear. It *was* much more becoming." She ventured a faint smile. "But I have to hide the scars, you know. I didn't care when there was just a little one, but now—here, look." She lifted her hair and started to turn.

Meli shuddered. "Oh no, I can't. It makes my skin—excuse me."

"Nonsense, you silly. All right, I was only asking you about the color anyway. You don't think it's too harsh?"

Meli answered without looking. "No, it's just the same."

Olga returned to the mirror and noticed that her mouth had moved into the frozen half-smile she had begun so to dislike. She promptly tried to purse her lips into a more serious expression.

"Very well, we're wasting too much time. I noticed a spot on my suede bag. See if you can brush it out."

Yes, the color is indeed good, Olga thought. *A dead, ashen blonde, quite suitable—almost like a natural blonde that has started to fade.* She thought of Contessa Narducci and had to push the smile back from her lips. *Forty years of black dye. What a horror! Well, she'd surely be there for the investiture this morning.* She had a vivid image of Narducci's red scalp, clearly visible beneath the teased, gauzy network of jet. She tilted her hat over her own hair smugly and peered at her watch. She couldn't make out the time distinctly and walked to her vanity table to consult the pink mother-of-pearl alarm clock there.

"Meli, forget the bag and call for a taxi right away. The way things are these days, even at the Vatican you can't be sure of a good seat unless you get there early."

"Really? But you have your invitation. I thought seats were always reserved for those who were actually invited."

"Just a few rows in front for the families and some

officials. The rest of us have to find seats wherever we can. You know how democratic the Church is these days."

Meli was already padding off to the foyer to call a taxi. She kept two spongy cloths a foot square just outside Olga's bedroom and shuffled along on these whenever she left, in order to polish the marble floors as she went through.

Olga checked the contents of her purse and found that her handkerchief had a large lipstick smudge on it. She tossed the soiled handkerchief to the floor of the closet and returned to her dressing table for another dab of toilet water before leaving. *I'm edgy as a cat this morning.* Her fingers sought the neck of the toilet water bottle with the stopper, fumbled, and knocked the bottle to the floor where it rolled, unbroken, spilling its contents over the marble.

"Oh damn." She glared at the fallen bottle.

"Let it alone. I'll get it." Meli rushed across the room and straightened the bottle, capped it firmly, and started to mop the spilled cologne with the handkerchief. "There's no damage. It didn't get anywhere near the rug." She gave a final swipe to the marble floor the table rested on. "I keep such a heavy coat of wax on the marble even the alcohol can't get through."

Olga had already left the room, not overly interested in the details of Meli's domestic occupations. She paused in the entrance hall to fluff a bunch of anemones in a vase.

"By the way, I'm expecting a guest this evening before dinner, but I doubt that he'll stay very long. He's from Matera but I doubt you know him; old Maresciallo's son Riccardo."

"But of course I know him. I mean, I remember him when he was a baby. How is he?"

"Never mind. As I was saying, I doubt that he'll stay very long, and please don't detain him with any stupid gossip about Nebbia. I think I'll receive him in my room.

There's less chance of his lingering too long that way. Now remember I have the Chinese reception first. You'll be here when I get back from that, won't you?"

"Oh yes, I stay till nine this evening, although—if your guest doesn't stay very long, perhaps I could leave at eight-thirty tonight? My mother is far from well."

"She's just old. All right, we'll see. If the house is all done you can leave as soon as he goes. Now be sure to get some rest before I get back from lunch."

"But I have all your laundry."

"Well, work fast then and get some rest afterwards. You look tired."

"Thank you, Contessa. The taxi number is Genoa thirty-two. You'd better go down now. They don't wait around any more."

"Genoa thirty-two?"

"That's right."

She stood patiently in front of the car door and repeated, "Genoa thirty-two?"

The driver was slumped behind the wheel as if he had been waiting a long while, and he crooked his neck slowly around to look at her. "I said yes."

"It is I who have engaged your services. Get out and open this door for me at once."

The driver colored behind his three-day-old beard and scampered out of the cab quickly. "Excuse me, *Signora*. I wasn't thinking. No one expects it any more, you know." He was about forty, with a burly frame and short, thick hands.

Olga glanced at the dirt under his nails as he opened the door and curled a nostril. "I do. And what is that disgusting odor?" She brushed his arm away as he appeared about to attempt to help her in.

"It's not the taxi, *Signora*. It's coming from across the river."

"Across the river. It's going to stink up the whole city.

St. Peter's Square please. The Scala Santa entrance. It smells like someone's burning rubber."

"That's just what it is, *Signora*." The driver seemed good-natured but kept glancing at her nervously through his reflector. "They're burning cars again. Two Volkswagens and a Mercedes, I heard. It's over in the center of Piazza Augusto Imperatore, right in front of San Carlo."

"Who is it this time?"

"Well, since they were all German cars I guess it must be the Red Brigades. They're still avenging Baader Meinhof."

"So they burn cars. The idiots."

The driver shrugged. "At least it's better than killing people."

"You approve?"

"*Signora*, how can I approve or disapprove? It's just something that's happening, that's all. Can a man disapprove of a rainstorm because he gets wet?"

"A man can stay dry or stand out in it and get soaked."

"Please, I'm too simple a man for politics. And I can see you are a philosopher." His eyes narrowed craftily. "I'm from the country, from Frosinone. A *sciosciaro* doesn't know anything about politics."

"Don't give me any of your sly nonsense. The further an Italian is from politics the more opinions he has about it. Would you mind closing your window, please? The breeze is driving that smell right in here."

"Yes, of course." His eyes glinted cunningly again. "When the wind comes from the east. . . . It's a strong wind. It will sweep all over Rome."

She was silent for a moment. "The wind from the east, eh? And you aren't political? Do you take me for an infant?"

"But it *is* a wind from the east." His voice was only faintly mocking.

"Stop thinking you're so damned clever. You're not being even faintly original. In the seventeenth century they called Protestantism the wind from the north, and it, too, was supposed to sweep all over Italy. You know how far *that* wind got. Really, the presumption!"

"Did I offend you, *Signora*?"

"Certainly not. I just find metaphors tiresome, particularly when someone quite stupid thinks he's being so terribly bright. Are you a Communist? I understand most cab drivers are."

"Are you a Fascist?"

"Don't be impertinent. If you wanted to ask me that you could have done so before I asked you whether you were a Communist. Oh, never mind, you're quite right. It's none of my business."

"Well, it's clear you're not a Communist."

"I'm not, of course, but I'd join the party tomorrow if I thought I had any chance of ruling in it. It's all the same, you know, masters and slaves."

"Everyone should be his own master."

"How touching. No, not in this world, my dear. *You* will always have a master, but I must say I find your simple faith charming. A couple of hundred years ago you'd have made a superb Christian. Perhaps you'd even have chosen to tend the garden in some quiet monastery."

"I am a Christian."

"Oh I know, I know. Tell me more about those cars they fired. Was anyone hurt?"

"I saw the whole thing. Or almost. I got there a few minutes later. I'd been taking a fare to Piazza del Popolo and you could hear something was going on. There was a German tourist with an Italian boy in the Mercedes. He said he had been hit by them when they pulled him out of the car, but there was no blood."

"Thank heaven for that. Slow down, will you. You mustn't race across the *piazza* like that. You almost hit those nuns."

"Excuse me, *Signora*. But they say that if I killed them

they would go straight to Paradise, isn't that so? Perhaps I was meant to be the heavenly instrument to deliver them to their reward."

He braked abruptly as they reached the colonnade outside the Scala Santa and rushed out to hold the door open for her. He bowed gravely and then gave a good-natured, yellow-toothed grin. "Better hurry, *Signora*. The Pope is waiting for you."

Olga paid him and then added three times the customary tip. "Up your ass."

He bowed even lower. "And a very good morning to you, too, *Signora*."

Meli picked through the heap of clothing that lay scattered across the laundry table, selected a dozen garments that looked like they had scarcely been worn, and sniffed them carefully. Then she put them in a separate pile of clothing to be ironed but not washed. She paused and drew herself up straight, holding her right side with both hands and pressing her fingers into the fleshless cage beneath her waist. She drew off her apron slowly, shaking her head, and went into the Countess' bedroom. She hesitated only briefly before she selected a bottle, put a drop of scent behind each ear, and went out.

Bar Marinetti had a large U-shaped service counter where most people took their coffee and *cornetti* and two booths tucked into a far corner, half-hidden by displays of boxed sweets and pastry. Meli headed for the far booth where three women her age were seated around glasses half-filled with dark brown liquid.

"You're late, Meli. We saw the old girl leave half an hour ago."

"Ah, there's so much to do. The older they get, the more demanding they are. I don't know how I go on. My liver is acting up again terribly today. I think I have complications."

"Maybe you should have a Rabarbaro for a change, or

maybe a Cynar." The woman who spoke had fierce dark eyebrows that joined across the bridge of her nose and were echoed lightly in the furry line above her lip.

"Thanks, but no, Nunziata. Those are good for you with your stomach, but Petrus is the only thing that helps my liver."

The barman had already poured a glass for Meli and she retrieved it before she sat down. She sipped it and scowled. "God, how bitter. But I hate to think what life would be like without it. No, of all the *amari*, Petrus is the only one that's made strictly for livers like mine."

A woman even smaller than Meli, with lips so thin they seemed to have been sucked forever into her mouth, shook her head solemnly. "Petrus is even better for appendicitis pain. When my *signora*'s mother was visiting two years ago she had an attack of appendicitis that nearly killed her. For two days she was in terrible pain and we were sure we would have to take her to the clinic. Then the electrician came by to fix the hot water heater, and he insisted they give her a small glass of Petrus every half hour." She sniffed to punctuate her dramatic pause. "The pains stopped that very night and never came back. Now the old woman takes it every day and she's nearly ninety."

Meli seemed to be weighing the merits of this argument. "Pippí, I didn't say Petrus was *only* for liver. I said *strictly* for liver. Everything that's put in it is made just for the liver, but that doesn't mean it can't help other conditions. Besides, the appendix and the liver are connected, you know."

"That's right," said the third woman. Faustina was stocky and sat with her legs spread wide, like tree trunks that had rooted on the spot. "Look at Fernet. Everyone says Fernet for an upset stomach, but the *signore* takes it when he has a headache or in the morning when he's had too much to drink the night before. And if a baby keeps crying all you have to do is give it some warm milk with two spoonfuls of sugar and a few drops of Fernet and it stops right away."

"Well, Fernet," said Nunziata. "It's all right if you can stand that poisonous taste. Maybe it is better, but Rabarbaro does just as well for my stomach and it doesn't make me nauseous."

"True," Faustina agreed. "Fernet helps my dizziness but I can't stand it either. The Averna works fine and the taste is so much better."

"But you'd better be careful, Faustina," said Pippí. "If you take Averna when you're having women's problems it increases the cramps. You have to switch to something neutral like Campari."

"Well, none of us has to worry about that anymore. But Campari is better for young women generally. From fourteen to forty are the Campari years."

"What was that awful smell on the streets when I got here?" asked Meli.

"Riots on the other side of the river. An American was dragged from his car and beaten half to death before his wife's eyes. She was pregnant and they had to rush her to the hospital where she was delivered of a premature baby marked with blood all over the right side of its face."

"Disgusting."

"Don't they have mothers?"

"Well, the other side of the river. What can you expect?"

"Who did it?"

"The N.A.P."

"The B.R."

"The G.M.S.I."

"Who gives a damn? What's the barman saying to that fellow at the bar? I don't think I've ever seen him before. They're looking this way."

"He must be asking for information."

"You know that barman. He always tells them, "Go ask *le zanzare*. The mosquitoes. Us. See, he's coming over."

A man in his twenties, wearing well-cut jeans and a knit shirt, approached them, smiling appeasingly. "Good morning, ladies."

"Good morning." They stared at him curiously.

"I was told you ladies might have heard of an apartment available somewhere in the neighborhood. Controlled of course."

"Sure, an apartment. You must be kidding."

"Nobody ever moves from here."

The man was careful not to relinquish his smile. "Please think. Perhaps you've heard of someone dying or going away to work in another city?"

Faustina turned to Pippí. "The daughter of Dentist Cavacallo moved her wedding day up a month. You can guess why." Then to the young man, "No, there's nothing."

"Perhaps I can buy you ladies a drink while you're thinking."

"We don't drink," they answered in chorus.

"Well, whatever it is you're having."

"Petrus, for my liver."

"Rabarbaro, for my stomach."

"Averna, for my dizziness. It comes from the pancreas."

"Cynar, for my bile."

"Fine, fine." He signaled the barman to pour the drinks.

Pippí drained her glass to make room for the next one. "You know, the son of Accountant Vitterini went to Genoa three months ago and he hasn't come back. Lisabetta the Lame said the landlord hasn't been paid in two months now. It's possible he's getting ready to reclaim the place, but it takes such a long time to do it."

"Where is it?" the young man asked quickly.

"Well, for one thing, it's furnished, you know. That means the landlord can raise your rent any time he feels like it. Are you sure you know what you're getting into?"

"Just give me the landlord's name and address, please. The least I can do is speak to him."

"I don't know. I hate to think of that nice young boy losing his apartment. I wonder why he didn't write the landlord, at least to say he'd been delayed. You'd think he'd know better with apartments as hard to get as they are. All right, give me a pencil." Pippí laboriously printed an address on a paper napkin and handed it to him. "It needs a new electric heater, there's a leak that comes from upstairs on Wednesday mornings, and one of the windows in the rear is cracked, but they just painted it last year and the rent is only 200,000."

"Wonderful. How many rooms are there?"

"How should I know? I've never seen it."

"Barman, another round of drinks for the ladies. Thank you." He dropped some money on the bar and raced out.

"I'm not sure I should have another one," said Meli. "I have to go buy some floor wax and when La Sarda sees me she always makes me have a Petrus with her because she suffers with the liver too."

"Go on. It can't hurt you."

"Maybe I should. It's worse today than it's ever been. My head feels it too."

"Then drink. It'll help. You should have another one after your lunch with a large glass of mineral water. San Pelegrino is best. Does the Countess have a bottle upstairs?"

"Of course. She keeps everything. I don't like to take medicine when I'm alone, though. I'd better go now. I think that burning smell outside has upset my digestion. I need to walk a little."

She rose slowly and walked toward the door, then stopped there and stood still for a moment. Faustina rushed to her.

"Meli, what's wrong?"

Meli looked at her a long time before she spoke. "Where did I say I was going?"

"Never mind. I'll walk you upstairs. You'd better lie down."

The investiture of the novice Swiss Guards was to take place on one of the open terraces near the pavilion, used mostly for the Pope's private, meditative promenades. It was the bleakest expanse of concrete in the Vatican, with accommodations for guests removed as far as possible from the balustrade with its delicious view of the gardens below. Once there had been cheerful pots of geraniums sentried about it, but it had been observed that after every public function held there, the geraniums were thoroughly denuded by the faithful to bless their own gardens or window boxes at home. Although the sky was cloudy, the light had the clear June brightness that would seem capable of warming even the grayest day in Rome. But there it was instantly absorbed into the remorseless concrete.

Although Olga had arrived quite early, the people already there had claimed nearly all of the first rows of folding chairs. They appeared to be mostly parents of the novices: the mothers wearing precisely the same dresses they would have chosen for their sons' weddings, and the fathers wearing the sober business suits to which they entrusted most of their days. There seemed to be twice as many mothers as usual, Olga observed, and far fewer clergy. And the Guards she could see standing about certainly weren't up to the old standards.

Her practiced eye had chosen a suitable seat the instant she entered the terrace, but she had to brush past a woman wearing a corsage trimmed with pink ribbon to reach it. The woman beamed at her, exuding Swiss *bonhomie*, and started to comment on the weather. But Olga dropped her eyes and headed for a chair a bit further to the side than the one she'd aimed for.

The row of seasoned Guards standing in the center of the terrace seemed a suitable focus for her attention, and she scrutinized them one by one as she waited for the ceremonies to begin.

They never used to let them get fat, she thought. *No discipline anymore.* Her memory slipped back to the morning of the first investiture she'd attended, and how slyly the guards had flirted with her. A glance held for a fraction of a second longer than necessary was quite enough in those days. Yes, they were certainly much better-looking then, although perhaps not quite as tall: leaner, harder, and more elegant. Surely from better families.

There must, nonetheless, be something attractive about their virginity, she decided, decidedly much more attractive than what one occasionally might feel about a young priest. Perhaps it was because their virginity was a temporary contract. She'd heard of some of them marrying, but it seemed that they were only given permission to do so after at least ten years' service. Still, this group! She sniffed, recalling recent times when she'd passed Guards on duty and seen them surrounded by young girls, not always tourists, who were flirting quite openly, even outrageously, as if they didn't know or didn't care that these were very special young men. And the Guards actually responded—talked to them, no doubt even made plans to meet them somewhere in wilful disregard of their vows of chastity. At least, she *supposed* they took vows of chastity, although of course they wouldn't be held to them quite as strictly as would be a priest. Still, a vow is a vow, and if they wanted to behave like tomcats they shouldn't have chosen the Swiss Guard. They were, after all, the dedicated protectors of the Pope. Surely their responsibility was to remain aloof from any hint of carnality. Her eyes scanned the line again, wondering how many of them might still be virgins. *None,* she decided, *not one,* and stiffened her back against the wooden slats of her chair.

She had a brief impulse to turn to see who might have

arrived, but she checked herself in time. It was a matter of principle with Olga to take her seat as quickly and inconspicuously as possible and never, never to turn to acknowledge an acquaintance until the ceremony had ended. That, after all, was what the reception period was for. She glanced down her nose at the woman chatting volubly in the row ahead. How badly people behaved!

A bishop with a thin voice stood before an inoperative microphone and started delivering a message that could not have been heard even if, by odd chance, one were curious enough to wish to listen.

The only occasion that *one is ever allowed to speak*, Olga thought maliciously, *is when someone must fill in time before the rest of the guests arrive.*

She was quite right, and the bishop was inwardly reflecting a prayer of thanks as he spoke, grateful that he could deliver his favorite speech, suitable for so many occasions, with scarcely any alterations.

The second speaker was an officer of the Swiss Guard who snapped the microphone stand and clicked sharply at the instrument with his forefinger as he energetically tried to reach his audience. But after a few minutes his voice flagged and was lost in the whispers of the crowd.

The third speaker was a peppery, diminutive cardinal, a man who was recognized as one very close to the Holy Father. He met with much more success, partly because he was preceded by an extravagant flourish of trumpets and a porter with a new microphone.

The ceremony was proceeding more briskly now and making sharper demands for attention. The guests squirmed and craned forward to peer at the novices who were taking turns presenting themselves to the solemn cluster of officers and clerics in the center of the terrace. They would march stiffly forward to be received, salute, march a few yards away, turn smartly to salute the audience with an elaborate flourish of their pikes, and then rejoin their ranks.

Olga threw her eyes heavenward. *God help us, they're*

worse this year than they've ever been. That little one! He looks just like the American comic, Woody somebody.

As soon as the thought crossed her mind, the recruit, as if on cue, swung around too sharply, lost the balance of his pike, and brought his hand to his cheek in horror as he watched the metal bounce with a sharp clang on the concrete. He retrieved the pike clumsily and shrank, rather than marched, back to his position.

The crowd buzzed and shifted in embarrassment, and a somber, cadaverous man who had taken a seat next to Olga cocked his head toward her ear. She did not move closer.

"It's an omen, a disaster. The Holy Father, I'm sure. I'm afraid he will not last out the year."

Olga arched her back slightly but did not choose to acknowledge his comment by a glance or a nod. Of course it was a bad year! And the Pope couldn't have that much longer to live anyway—but the stupidity of these people! To say things like that, and to a stranger. Such superstition, such lack of taste. Still, she considered, perhaps it was a sign after all.

The gloomy man was not put off by Olga's lack of response. "What a terrible time for a thing like this to happen. First the Red Brigades ignore the Holy Father's sacred appeal, and now—They say, I don't know what to think, that he will be the last Pope, that we will all go into a period of—"

Olga turned sharply. "If you need counseling, sir, I am sure there is a confessor here who will hear you."

The man's eyes searched desperately for an unoccupied chair nearby, but, seeing none, he clasped his hands as if in prayer, lowered his eyelids, and began to mumble unintelligibly but loudly.

The rest of the ceremony seemed vague and anticlimactic. Olga was grateful when people stirred to their feet and she could start to move towards the dais at the end of the reception center.

But where was Giulio? He was invariably at hand,

waiting to sweep her up before she'd barely walked two steps. She was irritated to realize she missed him. He wasn't much to look at, it was true, and his was not a very old or particularly distinguished name, but he *was* loyal, and she did like to appear to be escorted when she approached other guests. Just as she convinced herself he must be ill today, she heard a familiar wheeze and then he grasped her elbow.

"Olga, what a miracle you are."

She turned and looked impassively into Giulio's florid face. *His blood pressure must be sky high.* "Greetings, Giulio." She leaned her face forward for the formal brush of her cheeks with which he greeted her. "Will you help me find a cup of tea, dear?" *At least he isn't sweating yet.*

"There was no place to park. The whole Vatican is a garage today—but then I suppose that's true everywhere. I arrived just behind La Narducci. Have you seen her yet?" His eyes glittered mischievously.

"No, I haven't seen anyone."

"Just you wait, my dear; just you wait." He wheezed asthmatically and moved to the refreshment counter. Servants in Renaissance livery were pouring coffee, tea, and punch and offering frosted cakes to the group that was now thronging at that end of the terrace.

Once Olga had a teacup in her hand to toy with, she was able to assume her customary social demeanor, fixing a practiced half-smile on her face that looked pleasant enough and was to remain virtually unvaried until she left.

A woman with a large body that swayed uncertainly on very slender ankles and baby feet teetered toward them. She appeared to have increased her weight only recently, because her body was stuffed into the sausage casing of a chic, gun-metal silk dress, cut very low in front, that looked new. A light, crocheted *fichu* lay draped over the top of her bosom, only partially concealing the aggressive swell of pink, slightly sunburned breasts. In one hand she clutched a large leather purse, almost the size of an overnight bag.

"Olga, *dear* one. The only one I know who never changes. How *do* you do it?" There was only a hint of acid in her voice.

"Paola, dear. No, please don't kiss me. There are so many new bugs floating around Rome. How very well you look. Something obviously agrees with you. You know Giulio," she waved vaguely.

"But of course we know each other." Paola extended her fingertips, which Giulio leaned toward briefly. "We see each other often enough—but actually I believe my nephew is married to your cousin, the little Canotti."

"My wife's cousin."

"Well, same thing."

"Not at all. I haven't seen my wife in years. But I do admit her cousin is charming. I believe I saw you last April at the Viterbi, March at the New Zealanders, February at Cardinal Zenobbi, and weren't we both here last year?"

"Of course we were. Really, we should know each other better. Do you ever get to the Marches?"

"Rarely."

"What a pity. It's the only place I can really entertain. You know how hard it is with staff in Rome. By the way," she turned again to Olga, "have you seen La Narducci yet?"

Olga looked suspiciously at Giulio. "No, why?"

"Oh, you'll see."

"So I've been told. Well, I'm sure we'll find her soon enough. Giulio, will you be a dear and take me over to say hello to Doctor Asserato. I want to ask him about his daughter. I hear she's marrying the youngest son of Prince Lazzarone—the bright one. *Ciao*, Paola."

She whispered confidingly to Giulio as soon as they had placed a discreet distance between themselves and Paola. "It was definitely time to leave her. I saw her eyeing the pastries, and I'm afraid I still become embarrassed when she starts that business."

Giulio squeezed her arm. "There she goes. Look, she's starting."

They both turned to watch from their vantage point, trying not to appear too obvious, as Contessa Paola Stracozzi moved toward the display of pastry trays. Her left hand expertly opened the clasp of her large bag while her right hand swept over the array of *petit fours*. She appeared to hesitate as she selected a pink and chocolate cake between her thumb and forefinger; meanwhile the other fingers simultaneously closed around two more *petit fours* and pressed them into her palm. Then, as she withdrew her right hand, the left one sprung the purse open to receive the extra two pastries that were dropped in and promptly snapped the bag shut. Paola paused and started to nibble the remaining sweet held daintily aloft in her fingertips. She fluttered her eyelids and tried to appear to be chatting amiably with the person on her left, who growled an answer in German without looking at her.

"I'm very fond of Paola," said Olga, "but I simply can't bear to talk to her when there's food nearby. I understand she even has a new plastic liner for her bag that takes lasagna."

"Brace yourself, darling. I think that's La Caraviola headed this way."

"It can't be. I was sure she died."

"No, she's given up that hideous flat in Vigna Clara and lives in Portugal now. She says she couldn't bear to live so far from her King."

"Also, it's cheap, and no one knows her."

A woman of an age as indefinable as Olga's came toward them, radiating a harlequin smile. Her eyebrows had been replaced by two firmly painted black arches that rose well above her brow line, giving her a look of perpetual amazement. Her face was coated with a bright blush that had been inexpertly blended into the pale gray of her throat. She wore a beige silk blouse and matching trousers that hung loosely on her slender frame and suggested a remarkably attractive body that seemed sharply at variance with the drawn, painted face above it. Her hair was covered completely by a patterned scarf, and her costume suggested an impromptu appearance at the cocktail bar of a fashionable beach resort. As she drew closer, Olga's eyes were drawn to an irregular pattern of colored spots across the front of her blouse and trousers.

"Vera, I can't believe it. How incredibly well you look. Your figure! My dear, you have the body of a child." *That's tomato sauce, that's red wine, that's chocolate*, Olga ticked off. *And that*, she observed, glancing toward the trouser cuffs, *that could only be shit.*

"Olga. Beautiful, beautiful Olga. Oh, how happy I am that I let myself be talked into coming." She clasped the gloved hand that had been tentatively proffered and pressed it hard to her bosom.

Silicone, thought Olga. *The old tart.*

"Darling, I just came in from Portugal to see my daughter. She's absolutely miserable without me, you know. Please, *please*, promise you'll phone me this week. I'm dying to see you. There's so much to tell you." She paused and allowed her dazzling smile to rest on Giulio a moment. "Still the faithful courtier, I see."

Giulio bowed slightly. "You've been gone a long time. You'll stay a while now?"

"Oh, I can't, I simply can't. I have so many obligations in Portugal now. You can't imagine what it's like. Really, you should come there. *They* still have style. There are values. Morals. Yes, my dears, it's the only place left."

"Oh? I'd heard it was rather awful these days. Politically, I mean."

"But that's the rest of the country." Her hand swept airily upward. "Estoril, Cascais—they're still *ours*." She spotted someone past Giulio's shoulder and started to wave frantically. "Kisses, my dears, kisses. And don't forget, Olga, I'll be waiting for your call." She turned and walked briskly away, revealing a large discolored blot on her bottom, as if she'd been sitting in a puddle.

"Waiting for my call indeed," Olga sniffed. "Waiting for my invitation, she means." They paused a moment to sip their tea. "Giulio, why don't you tell me something of yourself? You know I've seen you three times this week and you still never tell me what you're up to."

He shrugged. "Oh, come now, you know my life as well as anyone in Rome. But before you hear it from anyone else, I suppose I should tell you my son's marriage is to be annulled."

"Oh, I *am* sorry."

"You sound like you've already heard."

"Of course I have. But don't worry, everyone is sure it's not his fault, and I never did care much for that little Austrian he married."

"Oh, but I did. She's really charming when you know her. A little inbred, of course—they'll never get rid of that chin—but still a very sweet girl. I'm glad people are saying it's not his fault, though. It isn't really. I mean it's not exactly a fault, more of a tendency perhaps. My father had the same thing. Thank God I was spared."

"Well, I'm sure it's all for the best. Think how much worse it would have been if they'd had children. Oh, dear me, I forgot. She was in an interesting condition the last time I saw her, wasn't she?"

He looked at her curiously. "How could you have known? She had just begun."

"I think she told me."

"Well, she's not now."

"That's a blessing." She took another sip of tea. "Oh my! Could that be? La Narducci? It is. Oh God, I see what you mean." She turned quickly and brought her handkerchief up to hide the smile that threatened to rise, then noticed with irritation that she had gotten lipstick on it. "More damn handkerchiefs," she muttered.

Contessa Narducci was approaching them, beaming. Her legs were extremely short in proportion to her torso, and to achieve a normal pace she was obliged to move them twice as rapidly as she would naturally be inclined to. Instead of her usual teased and blackened hair, her head was now capped by a massive wig of curly black pads that threatened to topple her by their sheer mass.

"Greetings, greetings," she chortled. "Before you say anything, I want you to notice my new wig. Yes, it's a wig. Truly. I decided it's just too much trouble fussing for hours every time I went out. You have to, you know, with hair as fine as mine. So when I found a wig I liked, and in my natural color, I jumped on it." She pirouetted for them. "What do you think?"

"I'm sure it's very practical." *She should have jumped a little harder.*

"Yes, and why not, I say. It's very modern. More and more chic women are wearing them. You should try one, Olga. At least for parties. They're so easy."

"Perhaps one day. Not yet." *Not even in my tomb, you cow.*

Contessa Narducci colored slightly and turned to Giulio. "And men are wearing them, too. They're very youthful, you know. You'd probably look ten or twenty years younger with one, Giulio."

"But I don't want to look any younger. Of course I enjoy ladies' making the most of their beauty, but don't you agree it would be pointless for me? What would I do next, trade in this nose?" He playfully tweaked his nose, which was bulbous and very red.

"You could these days, if you wanted to. Although I, for one, like your nose. It has great character."

"Thank you, and *I* like my hair—or what's left of it."

"But do you really like mine? I think a man's opinion is so much more important than another woman's. Come now, tell me if you don't. I promise not to be offended."

"Perhaps. Why not? Maybe even another color."

Narducci squeezed out a high-pitched giggle. "Ah, I

can see there's no point trying to keep secrets from you two. I've already *tried* another color." She paused dramatically and clasped her hands before her girlishly. "I wanted it to be a surprise. You're going to the Chinese this evening, aren't you? Oh, I couldn't resist. As soon as I saw how marvelous this one looked I ran out and bought two more. Tonight, my dears. Tonight you will see a new Narducci."

"I can hardly wait."

"*Ciao*, my darlings." She scampered off, waving her hands at a general she'd spotted talking to one of the new Guards, who now appeared to be backing away in less than graceful haste.

"I suppose there's a word for it?"

"Hydrocephalic?"

"You are too kind." Olga looked about her uncomfortably. "I've never seen more people I was anxious to avoid. Whenever you're ready to leave, I'd appreciate it if you'd give me a lift, that is, if you're headed back toward Parioli."

"I was going to ask you to lunch."

"You should have called. I'm having lunch with Gorizia."

"Mario? Oh really!"

Olga recognized the expression that reminded her so of a beagle. "You don't like him, do you?"

"It's not that. I don't find either his character or his outlook attractive. And he's too—too political, I think."

"We don't discuss politics. Actually, I'm going to return a favor. I have to interview one of those little girls he brings down from the country."

"Now of *that* I really do not approve, if you will permit my saying so."

"Those little peasants? He's very good to them."

Giulio's jaw tightened. "You shouldn't approve either."

"Nonsense. He finds them husbands and delivers them into a much better life. And with their virginity intact."

Giulio's tone became haughty. "Virginity is a technicality. What do you think he does with them in the house all the time before he delivers them to their husbands? No, I definitely do not approve."

"I'm sure it's none of my business, nor do I wish it to be. We're very old friends."

"It's not my business either, but I wouldn't like you to discover anything that might be uglier than you'd imagined."

"Dear Giulio, I'm not a child. Of course I know he amuses himself with those silly girls. And so? He has this rather quaint idea, old-fashioned, really. I suppose you'd call it a *droit du seigneur* with strict limitations."

"Limited by his morals or by his ability?"

"I never ask myself questions like that. Not even of you, and we're much better friends."

"Thanks, but promise not to become too involved. All right, I'm ready to leave now if you are."

"Just let me say two words—I see Cardinal Ciuffi and Archbishop Salem there, and they'd never forgive me if I left without saying hello."

As she moved toward the elevator in Mario's apartment, Olga noticed, as she always did, how much cleaner his entrance was kept than the one of the building she lived in. But then, Parioli was a much newer area of the city than Prati. Perhaps it wasn't really cleaner. Older buildings always retained more smell, more dampness, more stains in the travertine and more layers of gummy polish on the half-petrified wood. If this was cleaner, it was also a bit *arriviste*, she decided. Too many residences for all those embassies; over fifty new ones in the last ten years alone, she had been told. Too many newly rich, too many ex-suburban businessmen, too many aristocrats who had abandoned their villas for the simple conveniences of apartment dwelling. Abandoned them, in many cases, for a handsome price.

Well, it might be easy for *some* people to sell their villas to foreigners. One could get a fortune for any rustic horror as long as it was in one of the favored corners of Tuscany or near a major city. She'd been amused at the good fortune of some of her friends who had surrendered their huge, underheated, understaffed, and badly serviced villas to some pretentious foreigner who wanted to play *il gran signore*. However they were redecorated, one could be certain the crests remained.

She knew she could never have that luck with her own villa. Nebbia was a handsome, if somber, seventeenth-century building with vast grounds rich in olive trees, even if they didn't bear well anymore. But the closest city was Matera. It had over 40,000 inhabitants, but who, given the choice, would want to live near Matera? Foreigners seemed enchanted at first with photographs of Nebbia and Matera and appeared not to mind when she said the villa was millions of miles from nowhere. As a matter of fact, it was less than 200 miles from Naples, but only the most intrepid driver would attempt it in a day. It would have been easier if the villa were only a million miles from Matera. The first qualms arose when a prospective buyer learned that until very recently at least half the town's population had been cave-dwellers.

The caves were still there—dark, fetid holes that had walls cut out of the earth and were entered by trapdoor and ladder. Although most of the entrances had been blocked by concrete when the government moved the inhabitants to more conventional tenements, some of the more determined troglodytes found their way back, preferring to live with their chickens and even mules in the dirt-floor caves their ancestors had inhabited for centuries.

There might have been a few outsiders who could find this monumental squalor, unmatched in Italy, picturesque. Olga's hopes had been raised briefly a few years earlier when a Jolly Hotel opened to offer Matera's first accommodation to tourists. But any enthusiasm that could be generated by the picturesque vanished at the first appearance of the natives. They were, literally, frighteningly poor. Somehow the most wretched Neapolitans managed to look charming, and the most threadbare Sicilians made you at least admire their dignity. In Matera the children always seemed to have sores, so much easier to notice than their lice.

Once, just after World War II, Olga returned for a visit, and a distant cousin from the Veneto stopped by on her way to Taormina. She pretended to be charmed by the children who clustered around her with outstretched hands. The coins she offered were snatched greedily, but the children seemed reluctant to leave.

"I'm afraid I don't understand your dialect well," she told Olga. "It must be all the Greek words. Tell me, is *chini* a local word for candy?"

Olga nodded, too ashamed to tell her that *"Signorina, dammi u chini"* meant that the children were begging for quinine.

Their history had marked itself on their persons. The adults looked surly and hunted and constantly squinted in sunlight. Yet, she could remember individuals who were handsome and charming, even courtly in their manners. If only their dialect were more intelligible to outsiders. It was too much to expect them to learn anything else.

Of course there were some advantages. Labor was cheap. The cost of refurbishing Nebbia would be far less than would be required for many of the villas Olga had seen snapped up near Rome. But refurbishing Nebbia meant making do with the very basic materials and furnishings available in the area or spending a fortune to have something more attractive brought in.

Up to twenty years ago, refurbishing would have been the answer. Today Nebbia was virtually uninhabitable. Olga sometimes thought that it would still be a good place to go to die. While she didn't feel threatened by the thought of death, she was sure death must have a less secure hold in the bustle of Rome than it did in the brooding tranquility of Nebbia.

Her husband Gaetano had had no difficulty persuading her to leave Nebbia in 1929. Her father was dead and her mother was perfectly happy having the house to herself. Indeed, she never left it till she died in 1950. Olga had an older sister who married well, moved to Geneva, and never wrote again. Not that there had ever been a falling out. Communications just stopped, and it was clear she had no intention of returning to Italy or ever concerning herself with any of its inhabitants. Neither sister minded the separation very much, although Olga occasionally wondered whether her sister had had children.

Gaetano and she had taken the *piano nobile* in a fine solid house in Prati, with five marble baths and three reception rooms. It was only many years later, after Gaetano was killed in Ethiopia, that Olga could be persuaded by the brother-in-law who managed her accounts to take the smaller apartment with the charming terrace on an upper floor. But many of the finest people were already flaunting their straitened economies. One didn't want to be associated with the opportunists springing up at Mussolini's heels.

Prati was familiar to her even before she knew it well. It was the upper-class neighborhood nearest the Vatican, in spirit as well as location. The heart of the black aristocracy, they called it, and even today one could still hear in it the echoed heartbeat of black politics. The Reds had made scarcely any inroads in Prati. A bookseller in the next block showed some titles that were generally disapproved of by his clientele, but the graffiti on the nearby walls of the Tiber clearly defined where the area stood in its vote.

Parioli, where Mario and Giulio lived, stood just as far to the right as Prati. As she waited for someone to answer the bell, she thought of Giulio's words to her: "He's too political." Was he political? No, Giulio was wrong, she decided. Mario was simply a bit mad.

A girl about twenty who was still trying to fasten the strings on a stiffly starched apron opened the door and dipped her knee an inch or two.

"The lawyer is still in his room," she said. "He would like to offer you an aperitif there before you lunch, unless you would prefer the salon."

"Thank you, dear," said Olga, sweeping past her. She knew Mario was even harder to get out of his bedroom than she was.

"Hello, madman," she greeted him.

Mario struggled to his feet and looked puzzled. He rarely smiled, even when greeting someone he liked. "Madman? Why madman?"

The wall behind the headboard of his bed was covered with a giant photo of Mussolini's helmeted head. It had been there since long before the incursions of pop art. The other walls were painted alternately red, white, and green, with the Crown of Savoy in low-relief gold in the center of the white ground.

He indicated an elaborately carved, gold velvet chair and insisted she take her shoes off at once. "Antonietta, go fetch the Contessa a pair of slippers. Sit back, my dear. I like to feel you're comfortable when you visit me."

Mario had a slender frame, and not until he turned was the protuberance of his paunch noticeable. His trouser belt cut so deeply into his belly that it was fully covered by the fold of flesh that squeezed out over his waist. His hair was kept short, and his rather unremarkable features were half-hidden behind a pair of oversized tinted glasses in gold wire frames. Mario's lips had a way of pressing back and forth in an intermittent pout, and the nervous movements of his fingers increased the impression of petulance.

Olga wished there were a window open. "I don't suppose you have a Fernet? This is a full day for me, a hellish one, and it's always my stomach that rebels first."

"Certainly, darling. How were your Swiss Guards? Sexy as ever? I suspect half your pious Vatican friends go there to drool over the fresh meat."

She curled her lip. "I believe my stomach can answer that better than I, but I'd rather you didn't listen."

Mario twitched his shoulders as he produced some glasses from a little provincial cupboard on the Savoy wall. "All Swiss look like bank tellers to me, even when they're wearing funny trousers by Michelangelo." He gave her a Fernet Branca and poured himself a Rabarbaro without ice. "Do you mind if we have our drinks here?"

"Not if we could have a window opened."

He looked at her gravely. "Of course, of course. But let me move your chair first. You don't want a draft. Maybe I'd better get you a shawl. I have a lovely lace one of my mother's—"

She waved him away. "Nonsense. My great-grand-mother was Russian. You wear the shawl if you want to." She saw the hurt look on his face and quickly asked, "Tell me, how is your little educational circle going?" and instantly regretted the question.

"Marvelously, marvelously. Let me tell you, Olga, you must pay no attention to all the delinquents that get the newspaper publicity. There's a new spirit among the young today that's getting stronger, but you still don't hear much about it. The newspapers hardly ever write about it because it's not what the Red Bosses want to see. No matter. We have true patriots here in Rome who are fed up with the drug conspiracy and all the other techniques the Reds are using to corrupt our youth."

"That's nice. I'm glad there are still good boys."

"Good boys! Olga, these are *heroes* I'm talking about. Heroes! I've increased my history lectures at the society from two to three times a week and the hall is full every time. Such specimens! Athletes, intellectuals, serious Christians who want to restore this country to a position of respect in the world. Respect! Who respects Italy today? Nobody. But the change is coming. In ten years Italians won't be emigrating any more. They'll start coming back. You'll see. They'll come back from Australia, from America, even. They'll all want to be part of the new Italy because they will know they are respected."

"How interesting. Now—"

"And don't think we're neglecting respect for women's rights. Oh, no. That's an important part of our program, believe me. We honor the woman, first as the foundation of the home; we worship her, the pure woman who trains her sons, who teaches them respect for their country and for their family. What is Italian culture, I ask you, without respect for the family? It's the basis of our society."

"True, true. Just like the Chinese."

"The Chinese? Yes, of course. That's why the days of the Reds are numbered in China. How can you have respect for the family and accept a godless government?"

Olga stifled a yawn. "And your new protegée? When do I meet her?"

"She's in the kitchen now, working with Sara on our lunch. I don't know if she's intelligent; you'll have to tell me that. But she's a strong, healthy woman and will make one of my young men a wonderful wife. Thank God we got to her in time. She had started seeing a boy from a neighboring village, a factory worker, and you know what they are. But we'll reach them, too, in time—don't you worry. Anyway, I had her checked out before she came down and I was assured she is definitely all there."

"Do you suppose I could see her now, before lunch? I'd like to do this as quickly as possible. I don't wish to sound rude, but I'm afraid I'll have to run off right after lunch. I have an impossible day ahead of me."

"Whatever you say, my dear. Why don't I send her in to you now and wait for you on the terrace. Sara will put the pasta on as soon as you join me, and you can leave whenever you wish."

A few minutes later a girl of sixteen, more awkward than shy, stood in the doorway. She was unmistakably from the country, large-boned and open-faced, wearing a print dress and thick, patterned cotton stockings.

"Come in and close the door behind you, dear."

The girl did as she was told and took the seat Mario had vacated.

"I am Contessa Olga Seppi-Gianotti."

"Yes, Contessa."

"Well, and what is your name?"

"Anna. I thought the lawyer must have told you."

"Just Anna?"

"Yes. Oh, Anna Giuffetti."

"That's better. And you come from La Macchia."

"Yes, of course. The lawyer's town."

"And now you want to live in Rome?"

The girl nodded gravely.

"And I'm sure you want a husband. Well, the lawyer will find a good man for you, but you must do exactly as he tells you. Now stand up and let me have a better look at you, please."

The girl stood unselfconsciously and stared at Olga, then turned her body and held her face to the light when gestured to do so.

"All right, you may sit again. You have rather large bones, but even so, you're carrying a bit too much weight, particularly on the hips and thighs. Eat as much pasta as you wish, but have no bread with your second course, and never a dessert. No *cornetti* in the morning, either, and no soft drinks. How much sugar do you use in your coffee?"

"Two."

"Take one. In a week it will seem just as sweet. Now, we have to do something about your skin. First, I want you to go to the pharmacy this afternoon and buy this, and this, and this." She wrote hurriedly in a leatherbound notebook from her purse. "The lawyer will give you the money. Use them as the package says. You can read?"

"Of course."

"Fine. One product is to remove the fine hairs from

your lips. I know they're natural and hardly noticeable, but they aren't popular in Rome. The second is for your skin. It will clear it and make it smoother. Stop using soap on it. Water is quite enough. The third is a deodorant. You must use it morning and night. I think that's really all you need, except that you should shampoo your hair every day and brush it regularly. Shampooing will cut down the oils in your skin."

The girl was blushing now. "Every day?"

"Yes. I'll write it all down if you don't think you can remember. No? Oh, and while I think your hair is pretty, you might cut it just a little shorter here, and here. No need to go to a beauty salon. You can get Antonietta or someone to do it if you can't."

"Contessa, in my home town—"

"Yes, I know, the only girls who use deodorants every day are whores. But this is Rome, where whores set the fashion. Tell me, do you like the lawyer?"

"He's been very good to me. And my mother said I could never find a man I could trust more. He's found husbands here for a lot of girls from my village—much better than they could have found there."

"And you like this house? Keep your answers brief, please."

"Yes. It's a palace."

"Good. You'll probably live here for about six months. I shouldn't think it would be longer."

"You are very kind to take an interest in me."

"You must be kind too, particularly to the lawyer who is doing so much for you. He is a very lonely man. He never had a daughter, you know, and you must give him some of the affection he's missed. If you do exactly as I tell you, I can promise he won't hurt you."

"What do you mean, *hurt* me, Contessa?" Anna's eyes showed alarm.

"Do you trust me?"

"How should I not?"

"And you trust the lawyer?"

"Yes." Her voice hesitated only an instant.

"Very well. That's all that's necessary. The lawyer tells me you're a good girl. That's true, isn't it?" Her head made a slight jerk towards the girl's thighs.

"Of course." Anna was now crimson.

"You're absolutely sure that you've never let a man touch you down there, and that you've never touched a man?"

She shook her head vigorously. "Never."

"I believe you, but please understand that it is a point of great pride with the lawyer that you be delivered intact to the fine man who will be your husband."

Anna fidgeted with the edge of her sleeve but her eyes were fixed widely on her interviewer.

"In the meantime, the lawyer will teach you some things about yourself that will make it more pleasant for you when you marry." Olga dropped her eyes while she paused. "Tonight I want you to go to his bed." She raised her head and looked firmly into Anna's staring eyes. "I have already promised you he would not hurt you. It should give you pleasure. Use the bidet first; no one in the house will hear you."

"Oh Contessa, I don't want to make babies."

Olga stiffened. "I can assure you that's the furthest thing from his mind. That will come later, and only with your husband. The lawyer will only introduce you to the pleasure of being a woman. You will be made aware of your body. Have you ever touched yourself?"

Anna gasped.

"Well, it doesn't matter, but it would probably be better if he thinks you haven't."

"Contessa, I'm afraid."

"Nonsense. He will simply be affectionate with you. It's a delightful introduction to womanhood, and it may even make it a more pleasurable experience when you marry. I promise I'll come here once a week to see that everything's all right. I'm sure you'll be telling me how pleased you are."

"But why doesn't he ask me himself?"

"Mario—the lawyer, that is—is very shy, and he's afraid he might shock you if he ever discussed it. There will never be any mention of it made by him. That's another thing. There is no reason for you ever to discuss your relationship with him with anyone, not even the man you marry. Except for me, of course. If you ever have any questions, I'll be here to help you. Now, is it all clear?"

"I think so."

"And while you're in Rome, you must conduct yourself in public exactly as you would in La Macchia. By that I mean you are absolutely never to speak to strangers. There are many evil people who would try to hurt you if they got the chance—even to rob you of the treasure that is your guarantee of a good marriage. Guard it."

"Treasure, Contessa?"

"Your womanhood. There, between your legs. I dare say you'll know more about its power after tonight. Are there any other questions?"

Anna seemed reluctant to speak.

"What's the trouble? If there's something you want to know, now is the time to speak."

"Contessa, I'm not sure—I mean, I don't know *anything*. I'm so frightened. I don't know what I'm supposed to—I mean, what about his—"

"His maleness?"

The girl shrugged. "I suppose so. I've never seen a man before, but I've heard the women make jokes and they're supposed to want—things. They frighten me."

"Don't you have any brothers?"

"No. Just two younger sisters; my father died when I was six."

"There's nothing to worry about. I suspect you may never even get to see it."

"But what if I should? It makes me nervous. Are you sure I won't have to touch it?"

"I doubt it. I tell you it's nothing."

Anna was silent for a moment. "They're ugly, aren't they?"

"Not really. They just look like chicken gizzards. If that's all, you may go now. I believe Mario is waiting for his lunch."

Olga went out to the terrace and joined Mario at a table set under an arbor with a view of the park across the way.

"How much does she know?" he asked smiling.

"Nothing. I'm sure she's completely honest and anxious to please."

"Thank you, my dear. You would have made a wonderful mother."

"Nonsense. Anyway, I found her rather sweet. You should have no trouble getting her a good husband."

"Trouble getting her a husband? My dear Olga, I have the best young men in Rome lined up waiting. Where else could they find a virgin today?"

Meli had a warm bath waiting when Olga arrived home. It was almost four o'clock and Olga felt her knees were going to give way if she didn't get a chance to lie down at once. She was hurried out of her clothes and Meli gently eased her into the bath.

"Do you want salts?"

"No, just let me lie here. Did you have lunch?"

"A tomato. I can't eat much when it's warm."

"Neither can I. I felt positively ill, and I had to watch someone eat half a kilo of pasta by himself. Too sickmaking. Meli, bring me a Fernet, with ice please, and then go lie down. I shall want you to massage me later."

"Oh Contessa, I don't know if I'm up to it today."

"That's why I told you to go lie down. You look tired. Stay off your feet for a few minutes and you'll be fine."

Meli sighed and went for the Fernet Branca.

The water felt wonderfully soothing. Olga wriggled lower in the tub until the water touched her chin, and then she allowed her legs to float freely. She believed one could soak away years, soak away cares, soak away sins.

How she'd hated bathing at Nebbia. The water heater for her tub barely managed a couple of gallons of lukewarm water, and in winter she would splash the goose flesh of her skin and rub it frantically to keep from being convulsed by the cold. Never could she understand the cold baths that everyone else at Nebbia found invigorating. Whenever someone told her that cold baths were good for one, she never trusted that person again.

Here in Rome, everyone seemed to have all the warm water one needed. Even Meli, in her little flat out there in the western part of the city where she'd never been. More bathrooms than people, someone had once said of Rome. She wondered whether Mario would say that was why they had become soft. Personally, she preferred soft to hard.

Some of the distinctions in Roman society had seemed peculiar to her when she first settled in. She had been taught a strong distinction between the white aristocracy, which was her own, and the black aristocracy, with its titles manufactured by the Vatican. Her family had been landed for centuries and got its title during the first decades in which the Normans swept over that part of the peninsula. As a child, she had been taught that her title was distinctly superior to those of the black aristocrats she met. Her father established rigid classifications wherein even the finest black titles were merely a cut above the more than a hundred Sicilian princes created by the Spaniards during the seventeenth century. She had been assured that anyone with money could buy a title from the Pope. That a title could have been bought with equal ease from temporal rulers at most times was never mentioned.

Once in Rome, she found that the grandest aristocrats, even those who could claim a history longer than hers and those who lived most sumptuously, were all black. And her husband, another white aristocrat with a good, early-Renaissance title, seemed to acknowledge the superiority of the well-established black aristocrats they met.

The first blow to her pride came when she realized that people seeing her address in Prati were inclined to group her with those aristocrats who had wangled their titles only within the last century and settled into the reassuring environs of the Vatican. She remembered once hearing the phrase *una Contessa del Vaticano* cuttingly used to imply that the person referred to was little more than a genteel bourgeoise. After a while she didn't care. The rich had inherited the earth, and a title didn't even guarantee a good table in a restaurant anymore.

In Matera her rank was unquestioned, but still—she thought of some of the country aristocrats she knew there and decided that a clerk in Rome probably had more comforts. Cities had the money, the technology. It wasn't people who pampered you any more—it was science. Science meant modern, urban living with warm water; science meant pleasure; it meant—

She allowed her hands to caress the smoothness of her face and shoulders, then held them forward and shuddered.

"Damn," she said half-aloud. "Modern science be damned."

Tissues could be pulled and lifted, the pouches beneath her eyes removed, her cheeks smoothed, her breasts reshaped, her nipples relocated; even the little girdle of fat that had started to form around her middle some years ago had been sliced deftly away. But her hands! She looked at the wrinkled yellow claws covered with liver spots. "Damn these hands."

The surgeons always seemed impatient when she complained about the limits of their skill. Perhaps, they soothed, one day a colleague would succeed in widening the scope of their profession to include successful rejuvenation of the hands. Meantime—wear gloves.

And so she did. But when the gloves came off! How could she bear to look at the ugliness that was beyond anyone's ability to change.

Well, we'll see about that. Tonight, she thought. *There are still the old ways.* She felt comforted and stretched in the tub.

"Meli. Are you through resting?"

"What, Contessa?" a foggy voice answered.

"Come give me a good rub," she called. "I won't be able to nap unless you work some of this tension out of me first."

Meli came in barefoot and holding a large bath sheet and proceeded to pat her dry.

"On your laundry table, Meli. I think I need a really good pounding today."

"But Contessa, my arms are so sore, and I still have all your laundry to do."

"Try to use your back muscles more, then. Oh, come on, Meli—just a little while. I could scream right now, I'm so tense. Please, and then you can go lie down again while I take my nap. I promise I won't bother you again all day."

"But I have all the ironing and shopping. I have to carry all that mineral water."

"Oh, Meli." She had already spread a pallet on the table and climbed on it.

Meli sighed and began to knead Olga's neck and shoulders.

"Oh Meli, darling, that is so good. What would I do without you?" Under the firm pressure of Meli's fingers she felt herself almost slipping into sleep.

She felt the fingers stop their work and turned to see what was wrong. Meli's face was contorted and her mouth was opened as if screaming, but there was no sound. "What in the world—"

"It's my back. I think I threw something out." Meli had turned ashen and her thin lips were quivering uncontrollably.

"Oh, go lie down then. No, don't worry about me. I can look after myself, thank God."

Meli held her back with one hand and supported herself, panting, against the table.

She gulped in air and spoke hesitantly. "I creamed your rubber gloves. They're on the vanity table with your chin strap."

"Never mind. That stupid cream doesn't do any good anyway. These cosmetic companies are all out to rob you blind. All right. Go lie down, Meli, but be sure to wake me before five-thirty for that bloody reception. Damn, that's barely an hour. Well, what are you waiting for? I said go lie down."

Meli's eyes were darting wildly. "I'm afraid to move."

"Here, silly." Olga placed one hand firmly in the small of her back and wrapped an arm around her shoulder, gripping her firmly. "I'll help you. Come on. Move!"

Meli screamed and started to retch.

"Oh, for heaven's sake, stop acting like a sick cat. I'm trying to help you." She pushed Meli forward and then half-dragged her to the door of the utility room she used to rest in. "Now when you get home tonight, be sure to soak for an hour in a hot tub and you'll feel fine by morning."

"Yes, yes," she answered feebly and collapsed on the cot.

Olga hurried back to her own room, tied on her chin strap, looked at the creamed gloves thoughtfully for a moment, then tossed them back on the table and crawled into bed.

There's still lots of things they know more about in Matera than they do in Switzerland, she consoled herself, then promptly fell asleep.

At five forty-five Olga awakened herself and lay in bed for several minutes, squinting uncertainly at the clock on the dresser. Her interior sense of time eventually triumphed over her inability to focus on the clock, and she sat bolt upright in bed.

"Meli!" She tore off her chin strap and rushed to the dresser to verify the time. *Why the hell didn't she wake me?* "Meli!" There was still no answer.

No time to think. I'll wear the damned aubergine again. She flung open all the wardrobe doors, found her aubergine dress, gave it a quick check to be sure it had not been soiled. *I can do it when I have to but what the hell happened to Meli?* She entered the bathroom, opened the taps of the sink, and started rummaging through the medicine cabinet above. *Maybe she really was ill. I suppose I'd better look in on her.* She quickly fastened her peignoir around her waist and hurried to the utility room where she had left Meli on the cot. Meli had not changed position, but her eyes were open, staring at the ceiling. Her color was back.

"Meli, are you all right?"

"Of course, Contessa. Why shouldn't I be?"

The evenness of her reply alarmed Olga. "I think you'd better stay there until you're feeling better. Would you like me to cover you?"

"No, it's all right. I'll be getting up in a few minutes."

"Are you sure?" Olga twisted the belt of her peignoir. *I should have realized the old girl was really ill and set my alarm. If I don't bathe again I should be able to get there at a respectable time.* She reached forward and felt Meli's brow lightly with the back of her hand. It seemed cool enough.

"I'm all right now. I was just lying here thinking about Matera."

"Matera!" *Now I know she's not well.* "Would you like me to bring you some water? A Petrus perhaps?"

"No, nothing. I'd just like to lie here a few more minutes if you don't mind."

"All right. I have to dress now. It's getting late. Call if I can get you anything."

"Contessa, there is one thing."

"Yes?"

"Your laundry. It isn't done. Is it all right if I bring it down the street tomorrow? They do it for Contessa Sansevini."

"All right, Meli."

Olga returned to her bathroom and started the minute inspection of her face that preceded and followed every step in preparation for a social appearance.

Matera. How very odd.

Before Meli had come to Rome to work for the Contessa she had lived at Nebbia, where her mother was in service to the old Contessa, Olga's mother. There were no others in her family, and it was assumed—if it was thought of at all—that Meli would continue to work there as her mother had. Her mother was training her, and she tried to make herself useful to the rest of the staff when she was needed, although she was not particularly skillful in the kitchen and the maids resented her.

Through childhood and young womanhood, and into the bloom of maturity, Meli stayed on at Nebbia, never showing a particular inclination to depart from the routine of villa life. She went to church with her mother, visited friends in town with her mother, attended weddings and funerals with her, and observed the holidays, always with her mother.

Most of the men in Matera left for the north as soon as they were old enough to work. The marriage market was exceptionally competitive, even for a southern town. There were more than a few whom Meli eyed covertly, but none of them showed an inclination to court her. When her mother and the old Contessa tried to enumerate her assets on the marriage market, they never got beyond her virtue. And the women her age never found her interesting enough to ask her to the strictly controlled social functions they attended.

It was hard for the old Contessa to understand how she managed to get pregnant. When Meli noticed the interruption in her cycle she went to the Contessa instead of to her own mother to describe her symptoms. Her mother had never appeared either sympathetic or well-informed in these matters.

The Contessa was kind but interrogated her relentlessly. Did she have a lover? Of course not. Had a man forced her to make love to him? You mean, kissing and hugging, and all that sort of thing? No, no one. Make love? Was that somehow related to what the prefect had done? But no, he hadn't made love to her. He frightened her and hurt her but there was no lovemaking. Was she sure? Yes, but she had been very confused. Why would he want to hurt her? He must have struck her down there because she remembered there was blood later and she was sore, but he had never tried to kiss her or make love to her. Far from it; she still wondered what she had done to make him so angry with her that he would have wished to hurt her. Yes, that was the time she had stayed in bed three days with a headache.

The Contessa called in the midwife, whose gnarled hands prodded and hurt her even more than she could remember being hurt before. Where did it happen? Well, it must have happened when he had come to the villa on some minor local business and saw her on her way to the laundry house. No one would be at the group of utility buildings set apart from the central house at that hour. It was dark when she'd made her way back to the villa and she remembered wondering how it had gotten so late.

The midwife, a brown, smelly crone, confirmed the Contessa's suspicions. Not a maiden. And pregnant. No problem at all. She herself would perform the abortion the next night. If the Countess would pay there was no need to tell the girl's mother, or anyone else.

The prefect? A married man. And most of the population of Matera was directly indebted to him. As in most towns in southern Italy, it was the prefect or the mayor or chief clerk who controlled a large part of the town's cash income. Almost half the citizens of that province, the Basilicata, received a government pension of one sort or another for physical disability. The signed, sealed, and sworn statement of a local official, sent to Rome, eventually guaranteed an income for the rest of one's life—for blindness, for total deafness, for being without an arm or a leg. These officers were the town's principal benefactors, and one didn't lightly consider criticizing them. If you had a place to live you farmed for the food you ate and the wine you drank, but without the pension there would be no cigarettes, no clothing—nothing you needed cash for. According to the records in Rome—and the figures reached the tabloids but shocked no one—one-quarter of the population was afflicted with total blindness.

Meli had her abortion and was confined to her bed for six weeks fighting the infection that followed. Shortly after she was sent to Rome to work for Olga, and both she and her mother were granted pensions—not enough to last more than a week, really—but once they were certified as sightless they could always look forward to a monthly check.

As Olga was struggling to pull her dress over her head she heard a light cough and peered through the folds.

"Contessa."

"Yes, Meli. Come here and help me with this damn dress, will you."

"Forgive me, Contessa. It's only because I'm having my period."

"Of course, Meli. Now get my hairbrush and find some shoes for this, will you. And try one of the other taxi companies. Radio Taxi is full of Communists."

At six forty-five exactly the Contessa took her place at the end of the receiving line to shake hands with the new Taiwanese ambassador to the Vatican. The reception was being held in a hotel with an unprepossessing facade, virtually in the shadow of the Vatican walls. It held only a few dozen second-class rooms for pilgrims on tours, but there were two floors of spacious reception halls that provided the hotel's chief source of income. These could be divided into areas small enough to celebrate a first communion or be joined as they were now to accommodate a major reception.

Olga had already met the Taiwanese delegation at an informal dinner the week before, but this was their first formal reception. She found herself nodding to dozens of people as she waited her turn in the long hall. She could have compiled the guest list herself. Rome was, after all, a small town. A hundred people you spoke to, and a thousand you saw.

She murmured her way past her hosts and entered a larger room with tables lining the walls and light filtering down from six yellowed crystal chandeliers. The walls, the linens, the floors were in subtly varied shades that all recalled faded gardenia petals.

More than half the invited were already there, scattered across the hollow room and easily absorbed by the vastness. She hesitated only a moment, and then Giulio was there at her side, dressed now in evening clothes that had once fit him.

"How splendid you look. Let me admire you." He held her at arm's length while his eyes appeared to sweep appreciatively over the eggplant-colored satin that he had seen, she was estimating, about eighteen times a year for the last ten years.

"Aubergine is your color, my dear. It lights up your eyes. You should wear it more often."

In the morning they had spoken Italian. Now they slipped comfortably into English, since they knew it was to be the language of the evening.

"The Hungarians are here." She gestured toward a group of six stately guests, rather taller than most, who were nodding their way across the opposite end of the room. "I haven't seen them in ages. Odd they should show up for the Chinese."

"Perhaps this one plays bridge."

"I thought they all did."

"Perhaps this one plays badly."

The tables flanking the walls offered tray after tray of Chinese food, still a novelty in Italy. The unfamiliar delicacies were drawing a good deal of attention from the guests. A waiter passed them, and Giulio took two glasses of feebly sparkling wine away from his tray.

"I was told every Chinese cook in town was enlisted for tonight's affair, including some who work for the mainland trade commission. We must be sure to try some of those later. They intrigue me." He looked like he was waiting to loosen his belt at the first opportunity.

"Oh, absolutely. I adore Chinese food. Have you spotted La Narducci yet?" Olga preferred not to be seen scanning the crowd. "I confess I am curious about her surprise wig."

They stepped a few feet farther into the room and were instantly surrounded by a crowd of familiar faces exchanging traditional vacuities. A shrill cry of greeting pierced the murmured pleasantries, and conversation stopped while gesticulating arms froze in the air.

"God help us—it's La Narducci," someone whispered.

She waddled toward them, sheathed in gold lamé so tightly fitted about her hips that it hampered her movements. Her Brazilian shoes added several inches to her height, and a noisy gold necklace glittered and clamored for attention, but it was utterly overwhelmed by her dazzling wig. Row after row of fat curls rose in a plasticized gold pyramid flecked with gold dust, while two long, looser curls framed her face and dangled well below her ears.

"I told you it would be a surprise. Don't you love it?" Her swarthy skin was tinged crimson with excitement.

"It is most definitely a surprise," said Olga, "and quite unlike anything I might have imagined."

"And yet," added Giulio, "it is somehow so *you*."

"Thank you, thank you. Do you recognize it? Of course not. It's an exact copy of Dietrich's coiffure in *Flame of New Orleans* with Bruce Cabot, one of my most favorite movies. You see, I was just a child when they sent me to America, because by then the Fascists had started to—oh, excuse me, General, I didn't see you. Well anyway, it reminds me of the happiest years of my life."

"Ah, then that accounts for it," said Olga vacantly.

"Will we get *Blonde Venus* next week?" asked Giulio.

"Heavens no, that's too—too what?—*savage* for me. Oh, do come, I'd like you all to meet a very dear, dear friend of mine, a charming young bishop from Ireland. I think I left him somewhere over there." She jerked her head sharply to the side, and several people drew in their breaths as a cloud of gold dust rose from her head.

"Thank you, dear," sniffed Olga. "Only after I've eaten something, if you don't mind. Giulio, this wine is warm. Will you help me find another glass?" They walked a few steps away.

"So much for the side show," said Giulio. "It's time to move to the main ring. Do you know the Canadian woman standing there with all the emeralds? She's fantastically rich, they say. Building a new fifteenth-century villa on the Appia."

"Married?"

"A prince, I believe."

"Sicilian, I suppose?"

"I suppose. Come, I'd like to say a word or two to her. I hear she's putting together a fabulous cellar."

Olga was introduced to an aggressively attractive red-head in champagne-colored satin that was bias-cut to fall provocatively across the more prominent features of her body. The gown's straps were two thin bands of emeralds that passed unnoticed beneath the fiery display of a four-inch collar of gems fastened tightly about her throat. She was accompanied by a hawk-nosed, alert man, shorter than she but quite as striking.

"Call me Maggie," the redhead said. "I can't remember Italian names. It took me two weeks to memorize my own, and the prince here tells me I still can't pronounce it properly."

Her escort glared at her, bowed, and moved off without speaking.

Olga nodded her head lightly by way of acknowledgment.

"I like *your* name, though," the Canadian continued. "I'm Olga from the Volga. I can remember that." She laughed merrily at her own sally.

A liquid-eyed brunette with exquisitely chiseled features rushed up to them and grabbed Maggie's hands. "Maggie, darling. I'm so glad you're here. I was about to ring you before coming."

Olga nodded coldly to the young matron. Olympia de Sanctis was a Florentine baroness whose flirtations with leftist politics had been tolerated little better than her flirtations with leftist students. She was dressed in a well-cut denim suit and boots, not exactly appropriate to the occasion and certainly a bit too *jeune fille* for a woman in her mid-thirties.

"What the hell happened to you?" Maggie's voice was decidedly twangy. "You stand me up for lunch two weeks ago and I never even get a call."

Olga averted her eyes but made no attempt to leave. Unsuitable conversation was irresistible.

"Dearest, you can't imagine what a frightful time I've had. I told you how hard I'd been working with Giorgio." Olympia's eyes widened earnestly. "He has a new Xerox machine, and we'd been literally slaving, turning out simply thousands of pamphlets for that little club of his at school. Well, I tell you, we were both so exhausted I had to take him to Cortina for a couple of weeks."

Olga felt Giulio squeeze her elbow and turned to see a favorite of hers, Cardinal Briscola, who was holding court nearby for half a dozen women who appeared to be waiting in line to be presented and to kiss the ring he delicately proffered.

Olga turned to the Canadian, who still appeared a bit fretful with Olympia. *"Principessa*—Maggie, that is— would you like to meet my dear friend Cardinal Briscola? He is certainly one of the most entertaining men in Rome."

Maggie turned quickly and glanced at the cardinal, then at his entourage and the outstretched hand. "No thanks, honey. I don't stand in line for less than twenty carats." She turned back to Olympia. "Okay, forget it. Come around for lunch this Thursday, and bring Georgie if you want to, but give him a bath first."

Olga and Giulio reached gratefully for another glass of the warm Asti that was being passed again and moved away without being noticed.

Cardinal Briscola had finished with his attendants and swept the two of them off to the side for a few minutes of chit chat.

Certainly the new Taiwanese were very devout, a credit to the diplomatic community, and great philanthropists. That having been disposed of, Olga was able to turn the conversation to a more personal bent.

"And how is your nephew, Cardinal? I adore him, you know."

"Which one, Coco or Kiki?"

Olga hesitated only an instant. "They're both charmers, of course, but I meant Gianfranco. Coco?"

"Oh no, Gianfranco is Kiki. Ugo is Coco."

"Ugo is Coco?"

"Yes, that's right. He's fine, just fine. They both are. I'll tell them you asked. Will you come talk to me later? I see the new Taiwanese cardinal and I must have a word with him."

"Kiki and Coco," mused Giulio when he left. "And I have a niece called Chichi and a nephew called Bubu."

"It's revolting. All these young people acting as if they were ashamed of their very good names."

"Well, next year we'll be introduced to Pipi and Caca, no doubt, and perhaps that will end it. Are you ready for some food yet?"

They moved toward one of the buffet tables and selected plates.

"Oh dear, they appear not to have any napkins."

"Or forks." Giulio called over one of the waiters who was carrying out a tray of tiny spiced meatballs in a sweet and sour sauce. "Excuse me, I don't see any forks."

"No, of course not," the waiter answered loftily. "The Chinese don't use them."

"I see. Can you get us some forks, please."

The waiter seemed taken aback by what he decided was

an unreasonable demand. "But how? This is all catered. When we need forks we have to order them. Where would I get forks now for hundreds of people?"

"Two forks, please."

"At once, *dottore*," the waiter intoned, with the vacant expression that tells the experienced that the thought has been utterly dismissed from his mind.

"Oh Giulio, dear, you should have asked for two napkins instead." Olga remembered that she had discarded her lipsticked handkerchief earlier that day without taking a fresh one. She looked at the array of food, all the enticing tidbits either swimming in sauces or fried and coated with oil. She glanced down at the people standing with plates in hand, picking up tidbits with their fingers and popping them unconcernedly in their mouths. Her gloves would be stained. "I'm not hungry."

Two yards away Paola Stracozzi's oversized purse opened and swallowed half a dozen miniature egg rolls, then a handful of shrimp puffs. Paola glanced their way, recognized them, and came over at once. She was still chewing a large mouthful of food as she spoke.

"Greetings, you two. Olga, you must try one of these little rolls. They're pork in pastry. Simply delicious."

"Thank you. I think not." Olga was still holding an empty plate, looking for a place to set it down without being noticed.

"I insist. We can go to the loo later and rinse." She picked up a bowl and spooned out two wrinkled balls of rice paste wrapped around spiced forcemeat and placed them in Olga's plate, then spooned two more into her own. "There. And you must try one of these too. I can't tell what they are."

Olga shook her head firmly, but Paola put one on her plate, turned her back a moment, and set the bowl back down, now half-empty.

"Go on, I insist. But you must take your gloves off. You'll get them all greasy." She popped one of the little balls into her mouth and pursed her lips. "Heaven."

Olga's pale blue eyes glittered craftily. "I am afraid I cannot. I am told that in the classic recipe for this dish, which I am sure they would follow here, the chief ingredient in the stuffing is snake meat, which I do not digest."

Paola's jaws clamped down once more and remained fixed. She looked quite green and glanced down at her bulging purse as if it were a leper's bell. "But you must be joking."

"I never joke. Here's the ambassador now. Ask him if you don't believe me. *Eccelenza*—"

"Excuse me, but my fingers are sticky. I think I'll go wash."

Olga put her plate down and smiled at Giulio. He picked up a fried shrimp from one of the bowls. "Open wide, dear."

She accepted the morsel gratefully but demurred at eating another. "You're a treasure, Giulio. Forgive me now; I must leave, but I insist you stay a while longer. This all looks delicious."

"Oh, but it's early; you mustn't go yet."

"I have a caller coming by shortly and I don't want to miss him."

"Him?" Giulio feigned jealousy.

"You do become sweeter all the time. Yes, him. His father worked for us in Matera and he lives in Rome now. Does something at the Questura, I believe. He's been in Matera recently and I want to ask him how he found things. There's nothing as dear at our age as news of home."

"Thank you, Meli. I'm glad to see you've recovered. Please leave us now; we have some business to discuss. I'll call if I want you."

The man took the seat she indicated and perched on its edge as if he expected to be asked to fly. Although the summer had scarcely begun, he was already tanned to the color of a walnut. His teeth were white and even, his nose straight, his eyes wide-set, his hair a crisp black, and his body well knit. In short, he was a classic example of the prowling, virile Italian male more celebrated in legend than established in fact.

The Contessa turned the chair at her dressing table so that it faced him and sat quietly a moment, probing his face with undisguised curiosity before she spoke.

"I'd forgotten how very handsome you are, Riccardo."

"Thank you, Contessa," he answered with perfect ease. "May I say that you are still as lovely as my first memory of you."

She smiled and nodded. "Your father is well?"

"He doesn't leave the house anymore, but his compliments haven't changed. My sister takes good care of him."

"A good sign. And you. I can see you're fit. Are you still with the American?"

Riccardo decided to settle back in his chair. His smile had gone a bit crooked now. "Yes, but nothing will come of it. Our arrangement these days is that she comes to Italy twice a year, and for the month of March she brings me to America. They have a very nice villa with a swimming pool in Palm Springs." He automatically flexed his back as if to use his amply displayed bronze chest to illustrate the pleasures of the pool.

"But marriage, never, I suppose?"

"The senator would never hear of it. But apart from that, he doesn't interfere. It's not all too different from here, you know."

Olga cocked her head sympathetically. "I'm sorry. You had hoped, hadn't you?"

He shrugged his shoulders. "It was never more than an idea. Like a lottery ticket. But my work goes well. I'm a *sottocapo* now."

"Very good. And you'll probably soon be marrying a nice girl from Matera and starting a family. You must be almost thirty, no?"

"Just. No, Contessa, I've been away too long. And I never fancied a *fidanzata* from the *paese*. I could never be cynical enough to enter a marriage just to have a virtuous woman to run my house and have my children."

"Perhaps. But remember, none of us wants the same things at all times. Leave room for change."

She stared at him for a moment, and he didn't know whether he should try to resume conversation.

Olga straightened in her chair and clasped her hands. "Riccardo," she said softly, "did you bring me my opals?"

He seemed relieved at the break in that awkward pause and opened his shoulder bag. "Of course." He reached in and produced a cosmetics jar half-filled with a cloudy liquid and handed it to her.

"My dear boy, how can I ever thank you enough!" She stood to receive the jar, her outstretched hands trembling as they grasped it. She placed it reverently on the table and turned toward him, her eyes glistening with tears. "The money I gave you—are you sure it was enough?"

"More than enough, Contessa. It is I who thank you for allowing me to be of service."

She searched for even the faintest hint of a sneer behind the oiled phrase but decided he was merely echoing the old-fashioned courtesies he had learned from his father. "There were no problems?"

"Why no, of course not. What problems would there be?"

"I don't know. I can't imagine. What did you tell them?"

"Not very much. The truth more or less. I didn't mention your name, of course, but they don't care."

Olga assumed a more demure pose. "Please understand that I am also grateful that you didn't appear embarrassed by my request or allow *me* to be."

Riccardo's smile was devastating again. "Contessa, you must remember that my father used to perform the same little errand for your mother. As a matter of fact, the year before your mother, the saint, passed away, my father was very proud that I had been a contributor for two years, and I was still only twelve."

"My, you were precocious."

"No, just southern. The boys are all very happy to do it. I give them each enough for a couple of packs of cigarettes, but I don't even have to. And I leave them the magazines I bring for inspiration—as if they need it. No, they love it. It's an adventure."

"Charming, charming. And how old are these imps?"

"Between twelve and sixteen. According to my father, the benefits start to disappear after early adolescence. And your mother was very strict on that point, I believe."

The Contessa shook her head, still smiling. "I feel I haven't given you nearly enough for your services. No, don't say anything. I won't try to give you more money, but I'd like you to have something of my father's." She reached into a drawer and withdrew a small coin wrapped in silk. "This was minted in Italy's last year before the Republic. It's for accepting my commission as graciously as you did. It took me a long time before I had the courage to send for you, and I'm grateful to you for making it so easy. Thank you, Riccardo."

He reached for the coin slowly. "I take it with thanks, Contessa. It will be treasured as a reminder of a lady whom I have always admired." He stepped forward and kissed her lightly on the cheek. "And now I'm sure I have already taken up too much of your time. Please feel free to call me whenever I can be of service."

Olga had unaccountably begun to tremble, but she forced herself to be steady. "Let me see you to the door. I don't want to disturb my maid. She's been unwell today."

Riccardo turned just before they reached the door. He nodded toward the jar. "You don't need it, you know."

For what seemed the first time in many years Olga felt herself blushing. "Oh, but I do. I really do."

Alone once more at her dressing table, she held the jar to the light and watched the viscous fluid coat the glass sides as she rocked it gently. She carefully peeled off her gloves and unscrewed the lid of the jar. She hesitated a moment, staring at the surface before she tentatively prodded the sticky fluid with a finger. Why was her hand shaking so? She looked at the thin coating that glistened on the tip of her finger and sniffed it. At least there was no smell. She brushed her fingertip along the back of her other hand as if she were testing a new shade of lipstick. The corrugated surface absorbed it at once and she believed she could already feel the skin tightening.

She stared at the back of her hand, fascinated, and recalled an incident from her girlhood. When she was a child her parents usually took turns visiting her room to kiss her goodnight. But one night when she was just old enough to go to a party at a neighboring villa with her sister, she was still up some time after her parents had retired. She entered her mother's bedroom—where she was ordinarily never permitted to go without asking first—to kiss her goodnight, and her mother said, "No, you mustn't kiss me tonight, my darling." When Olga insisted, her mother told her she had her egg mask on and must never be kissed when she was wearing it. Olga leaned over and kissed her mother anyway, and not a word more was said of it till breakfast time, when Olga asked her mother what the egg mask was good for and her father stormed from the table. She thought at the time that her father was acting silly and probably didn't like the egg mask because he knew he wasn't supposed to kiss her mother when she had it on.

It wasn't until after she married and was leaving Nebbia that her mother showed her a jar of her cosmetic cream and told her that if she ever needed it she must ask Riccardo's father to get her some. "It's liquid opal. The hard stone is the female opal, but the liquid opal is male. You will find Sebastiano discreet. You must be too, and use liquid opal only when you know it is time. It's worthless on young women."

When Riccardo came to Rome he called at once to pay

his respects, and then occasionally she would run into him. He always insisted that he was waiting for the privilege of being of service to her, but she had at first dismissed his words as routine politeness. His words seemed carefully weighted as she thought of them now. It was clearly a mission he'd been expecting.

"Contessa."

Meli's voice startled her, and the fingers that had just dipped into the semicoagulated fluid jerked and knocked the jar to the floor. She gasped and retrieved the jar before it had discharged more than a small puddle on the marble floor.

"Don't trouble, Contessa. I'll get it."

Meli bustled over, untying the dish towel from her waist to wipe up. "Excuse me, Contessa, I didn't mean to—but! What the hell is this?"

She straightened and charged Olga with a look of passionate indignation. "Filth! You witch. Oh, I know what that is in the jar. Don't think I don't know. Your mother too. Witches, both of you. Everyone in Matera knows. They told me and I never believed them. Filthy witches. You sell your souls to keep young."

Saliva was sputtering from her mouth and she had started to pant from the exertion of her outburst.

"Meli, please listen to me. You don't know what you're saying. That was just a—"

"*I* don't know what I'm saying! What do you take me for? We both know. But I will denounce you. Wait and see. I will denounce you to everyone. There's nothing but filth in this house. Filth!"

"Please. Listen to me, Meli." Olga sat down and pressed her hands to her temples. She was sure she was going to faint.

"No, you listen to me. I've worked myself to the bone for you, the same as my mother did for your mother, and what do I get for it? You don't pay for my pension; you don't pay for my medical insurance. You think I don't know my rights? You pay me half of what the law says I should get, the *law*, and I never even open my mouth because you say you'll always take care of me and that nobody else would ever hire me at my age. Well, what have you or your mother ever done for my mother besides keep her alive so she could slave for you? A poor, paralyzed vegetable who just sits and drools at me when I go home, and sometimes I'm too tired now to even change her until morning. Is that how you take care of your own? Witch!"

"Meli, please. I'm not well."

"Witches. You and your mother. And now you're going to pay for it."

"Meli, you're being hysterical. Please. Sit down in that chair and listen to me." Olga was fighting desperately for control of herself. "You were hired long before the new laws about pensions and medical plans."

"Witch."

"We've always done things the old way. If you didn't work for me, where would you be? Just suppose I had let you go when the new laws came into effect because I couldn't afford you. Where would you be then?"

"Witch." Meli's body was rocking back and forth in the chair.

"And your mother. You know I send her something every Christmas, Easter, and *Ferragosto,* as well as on her feast day. You can't say my family doesn't take care of its own." She realized her speech was becoming slurred.

Meli jumped to her feet again. "Enough. You're filth and may I drop dead if I don't denounce you. And don't talk to me about new laws. They still apply to me no matter how long I worked without them. Don't you think everybody knows that? Do you think because we can't read, we're stupid? I'm going to leave you. What do you think of that? And what's more, I want my full severance pay."

"You can't do that to me, Meli." Olga was pressing her

throat hard with her fingers to urge back the nausea that was rising, and she knew she would be bruised in the morning.

"Oh yes, I can. I have one month's pay coming to me for every year I've worked for you. And that's not a new law; that goes back to Mussolini. You think I don't know these things, ha? Forty-five months, Contessa, and at the *legal* rate, not what you starve me on. And come to think of it, I want my mother's severance pay, too."

"Meli, let me get you a glass of water. You're frightening me." She hurried to the bathroom for a glass of water, grateful to escape for even a moment from the accusing eyes and the awful hate in that voice. Her hands were still trembling when she returned, rocking the water in the half-filled glass she offered.

"I brought you a pill to calm yourself."

Meli took the pill and hurled it to the floor. "What the hell are you trying to give me? More filth? We're simple honest people. We don't use your devil's things to make ourselves look young or feel better."

She drank the water in a long gulp. "Thank you, Contessa. Never mind. Forty-five months' legal pay, and I'm still going to denounce you."

Olga felt more in control of herself when she saw Meli drink the water. "Meli, dear, even if you were to leave me, you know I'd never stop the salary I was giving you. I've already promised you that. Why do you insist on trying to hurt me?"

"You're an evil breed. I'm through with you. I'm going to take the money and bring my mother back to Matera. You think I have no one? I have a cousin, a nephew. And nobody ever starves in Matera. The poor know how to take care of each other."

"Enough, please. I can't stand any more." Olga fumbled in her dresser and found two bills, then searched further and found two more and pressed them into Meli's hand. "Stay with your mother a while and take care of her. She and my mother loved each other very much, you know, even as I thought you and I did. I'll manage somehow without you for a while. Then, when you're rested, come back and talk to me. You'll see things differently, I promise you."

Meli's first impulse when she saw the money was to spit on it and throw it in Olga's face. But once it was pressed into her palm she felt her fingers tighten around the bills and then thrust them under her apron into a pocket.

"All right, I'm going now. But I meant every word I said; you see if I don't." Her voice was calmer but still husky.

She went into her cell and hung her apron neatly in the wardrobe, picked up her purse, put the money into a worn wallet, and then thought better of it and placed it in her bosom. She tiptoed out of the apartment, closing the door quietly behind her.

Olga sat on the bed for a long time. It was too early for sleep. *Really, I was foolish to let myself become upset by that ridiculous Meli. Mother would never have let the situation go so far.*

She rose finally and entered the bathroom. It was scarcely four hours since her last bath, but she ran the water and undressed mechanically, then kicked her discarded clothing under the sink.

Drawing the bath is Meli's job. She discovered the water was much too hot and testily turned on the cold tap. Minutes later she lowered herself into the tub and stretched her frame gracefully. The water lapped at her chin but her body refused to relax.

I shouldn't have given her so much money. With all that cash she might stay away a week. Her jaw tensed. *Or more. Could she possibly be serious about going back to Matera? And move that half-witted invalid of a mother halfway across the country? No, she couldn't. Still, there's no telling what's going on in that head of hers. All these changes! Even ten years ago she would never have dared speak to me that way. Maybe she's losing her mind. Yes, that must be it. Meli has always been a bit odd. These country spinsters! All that nonsense again this morning about her periods. But what's happened that could make her bite the hand that feeds her? Yes, of course she's mad—quite, quite mad. I should have seen it sooner.*

I wonder if one of Mario's older girls might be suitable. It seems to me there was one that was deserted by her husband not too long ago. I must ask him about it tomorrow. Yes, she might do very nicely indeed. She could probably live in, too, as long as there are no brats. Yes. Maybe now there could be some real service again for a change. I'll call Mario as soon as I finish my bath.

She shut her eyes and felt quite peaceful after all.

The sky was still light, but it looked as if it would rain during the night. The *tramontana*, the cool breeze that sweeps in from the Alps at evening, had already begun to scrub away the foul air of daytime traffic, and Meli felt it brace her. She walked briskly across the bridge to where she would board the first of the two buses that would take her across the city to the working-class district on the periphery. Her mother and she shared two tiny rooms and a balcony filled with tired geraniums that overlooked rows of warrens just like theirs, but Meli looked forward every evening to returning there. It was theirs.

Meli was feeling stronger than she had in weeks and started a mental checklist of things she might need to buy on her way home before the shops closed. Bah! She wasn't going to prepare dinner tonight. Not after the day she'd had. She decided to buy a roasted chicken at the *rosticceria* beneath her flat. Her mother would like that. Yes. Maybe they would even have some fried eggplant and *panzarotti*, too. No need to bother her mother with any of the business that had gone on at the Contessa's. It was hard enough getting her to understand the simplest things, and even then you couldn't be sure. No. Mother would eat and be happy and not ask any questions. It was better. Meli hoped she wouldn't have to clean her again.

It was already too much for her. A neighbor had spoken of the little home run by nuns just a half-mile away from the apartment. They could take care of her better than Meli could. Maybe. Not yet. Maybe when it was time for them both to enter.

Even at this hour there were no seats on the bus. Meli sighed resignedly and shifted her weight as the bus turned and lurched down a broad avenue toward the center of town. *How long these bus trips take! If it weren't for Mamma I could stay in my little room at the Contessa's and never have to bother with all this. Three hours of travel every day! Well, why not live with the Contessa? It's a good place. Maybe Mamma would be happier with the nuns now. At least there would be someone around her all day. And who knows? The Contessa might leave me her money when she dies if I've been living with her. At least the apartment, and that must be worth a fortune. Why not? Who else has she got to leave it to? I'm like a sister to her. She said so herself.*

There was insistent honking up ahead, and she craned her head to see what was going on. As soon as the bus had traveled another hundred yards it stopped in the middle of the avenue, while the space on either side of it was quickly filled by tiny cars darting and searching for an advantage. It was a common enough occurrence, and Meli was patient for another three or four minutes. The honking grew worse as cars queued behind the bus and added their din to the existing racket.

Meli turned, exasperated, to a woman of her own age and class who was standing next to her. "What is it? What's holding us up?"

"Boh!" The woman's shrug illustrated her infinite resignation in the face of one more urban crisis.

There seemed to be some sort of commotion in the street ahead of them, and then a man at the front of the bus turned and said loudly to his fellow passengers, "It's another demonstration." The passengers muttered and swore freely.

Up ahead at the intersection they could now see

swarms of people beginning to surge through the street.

"But what do they want?" Meli asked again of her neighbor.

"Boh!"

The bus driver turned and spoke to his passengers calmly and with genuine sympathy in his voice. "I'm sorry for the inconvenience, but it looks like we're going to be here for quite a while. I can't give you a refund, but if any of you want to walk as far as the Piazza del Popolo you may find some other lines just outside the gate there that are still running. It's all I can suggest." He then lighted a cigarette and opened a copy of *Corriere dello Sport,* signaling his absolute detachment from any further responsibility toward them.

"*Porco Giuda,*" swore Meli. "Should we walk? I could catch a bus to Piazza Bologna and then change again there. Three buses. Damn."

"Boh!"

Meli got off and walked to the next intersection where the procession was now fully underway. The crowd marching with little semblance of organization was almost uniformly dressed in American blue jeans. Young men with beards were holding their fists high and shaking them unconvincingly. Others held poles strung with red banners demanding jobs, peace, unity, schools, guaranteed this, and guaranteed that. Meli tried to make out some of the words. She understood what the hammer and sickle meant but couldn't decide what the demonstration was all about. She looked curiously and then indignantly at the young women among the marchers. They smiled more than the men did but seemed just as determined. *What a scandal,* she thought. *They probably let those men do anything they want with them.* The bodies pressing around her began to make Meli feel very warm and then a bit heady. Her ears had started ringing. She remembered the bills she had tucked in her bosom and clutched them. She knew about crowds.

There was a feeble old man near her who looked like he was standing only by grace of the people's bodies crowded around him. Meli addressed him, perhaps because he was the only one at hand who looked as bewildered as she felt. "But what do they want?"

"Boh!"

The masses of people around her had grown even more confusing, so she directed her next question more generally to the throng surrounding her. "Can someone tell me what's happening? What's this all about? Who is it?" The sound of her voice surprised her. It was louder and shriller than she had intended, and she noticed people backing away to give her room.

"What is it? What's going on?"

She pushed forward with her elbows and fought her way through the crowd till she was right at curbside. These seemed to be younger students passing by now, their step just as determined but rather lighter in spirit than the others. Meli tried to grab a young girl's arm but she pulled away and continued marching.

"What do you want? What's happening?"

A young man carrying a tape deck switched it on and the students began to sing, uncertainly at first, and then their voices were cheerfully carrying the tune of the partisan song, *Bella Ciao*. Most of them seemed not to know the words but were yodeling along good-naturedly. Once in a while one would turn to Meli, not noticing or caring about her flushed, confused expression as they articulated their *"Bella ciao, bella ciao, bella ciao, ciao, ciao."*

"What do you want?" She was screaming now. "Good for nothings. Bums." Her neighbors gave her a wide berth at the curb. "Why don't you good-for-nothing bums go out and work for a living? You rotten little bastards. You dirty sons of bitches. Go do something for your country, you whores, you—"

SEBASTIAN

NORMAN

Officer Norman Ashe signed out half an hour early and went for a walk on campus. It had been a troublesome afternoon. As a rookie he'd already had more than a reasonable exposure to violent crime, but this was the first time the victim was a person he'd known. And such an unlikely victim.

He ticked off the list of homicides he'd encountered before this. A wino with his throat slit in the park, a battered housewife clutching a swag of her assailant's scalp, a strangled hooker, three junkies, one of them aged fifteen, and then Professor Cheyne. Mild Professor Cheyne, laced with curiously bloodless cuts, yet still gentle in death. He remembered the face of the fifteen-year-old junkie with the angry purple blotches on his skin and the grotesquely contorted features. Cheyne's eyes were open, staring tranquilly ahead, and his features were composed. How could a violent death produce such calm?

The superintendent and his wife, Horace and Anna Anderson, had felt the wonder of it too. They had liked him, clearly. To listen to them, Professor Cheyne was the most unlikely candidate for sudden death; a quiet widower dedicated to his work. Their comments made Detective Hassler's speculations even more crude and abrasive. Norman realized he'd been more shocked by

Hassler's blunt opinions than he had been when he recognized Professor Cheyne's corpse tied to the bedpost.

He had never liked Detective Hassler. Whenever he worked with him it was an effort to restrain himself from telling him exactly what he thought of his theories.

Why would a thief neatly cut the canvasses out of all the frames in the rooms and not touch the money and watch that were in plain view on the bedroom dresser? Cheyne was not an important collector. The superintendent's wife was sure they were all his own paintings hanging, because she'd often seen him come in with rolls of canvas under his arm and had asked him about them. She had even glimpsed one on his wall once and said it was a religious subject. And both she and her husband insisted that Cheyne never had visitors and that he never brought men or women to his apartment at any hour.

Still, if anyone were to criticize Hassler's summary and often prejudiced conclusions, it had best be one of his superiors. Better for a rookie to keep his mouth shut. Much better yet for a Jewish rookie not to say anything that might invite another wounding look or cruel word. Maybe thin-skinned Jews didn't belong on the police force after all. Hassler would probably agree.

Dick Hassler was on record for his contemptuous attitude toward the younger policemen who had some college training. And then Norman Ashe had already admitted to him that his father had changed their name. As if that weren't enough, he had jokingly added that this was probably a good idea in any case, since most policemen couldn't be expected to spell Ashkenazy, and Hassler had not been amused.

Since it appeared that Hassler believed any education, however modest, was a handicap on the police force, Norman felt it was better not to mention that he had taken Professor Cheyne's lecture course in art history. Of course almost everyone at the University had. It was one of those basic requirements toward all degrees and there were hundreds of students at every lecture. Still, better not to mention it.

And any reference to St. Sebastian, however apt, would almost certainly have produced a sneering demand for *his* qualifications, of all people, to be making such a comparison. More like, "What the fuck do you know about saints?" How could he not have said something? With anyone but Dick Hassler there, he wouldn't have thought twice about it. The image of Professor Cheyne propped upright with his hands tied behind the bedpost, his body lean and hairless, almost boyish, with one leg lightly crooked forward, was a haunting one. It was precisely when the comparison to St. Sebastian crossed his mind that Hassler announced, "He had to be gay."

Norman felt that he could think more freely now that he had changed out of his uniform. Yes, it did make a difference. But would he be tempted to speak more openly to Detective Hassler if he were walking beside him? Could he challenge him here, on a University campus? He decided he couldn't.

This was a perfect evening for walking. The apple-crisp air of Minnesota's early fall enlivened his gait and he was soon in front of the neo-Gothic mausoleum where Professor Cheyne used to deliver his notable series of lectures on art history. Norman didn't pause but continued to walk around the building, sniffing his surroundings as if he were searching for something.

There weren't many people around. He glanced at his watch. The last class must have ended an hour and a half ago, but the libraries would still be open. He always looked for a familiar face on these walks. He had finished three full years at the University before deciding to become a policeman, and that was only seven or eight months ago. How odd that so very soon after he dropped out he should feel such an outsider.

The first time he returned to campus after becoming a cop, he visited the coffee shop where he could once greet half the people in it by name, and they were now already mostly strangers. Then one day he walked by in uniform, something he had hesitated to do, and when he greeted anyone, even students he had sat next to in class for months, they looked startled, jerked their heads in acknowledgment, and walked on. He had to admit ruefully that they didn't know him, that all they recognized was a uniform—and not a popular one at that.

Now, less than a year later, he hardly expected to see anyone he knew. Poor old Professor Cheyne. He was never certain the professor recognized him outside class. How could he? One face in a sea of blank faces that you addressed from a lecture platform twice a week, and a good deal of that time in a room darkened for the slide projector's review of buildings, statues, and paintings, guiding them smoothly from golden age to golden age.

No, and besides, Professor Cheyne seemed too shy a man to single out students for closer observation. Of course art history was different from most courses anyway. There was nothing more impersonal than those lectures. A review of American literature had been the same. The lecturer fixed his eyes in space somewhere just above the heads in the center of the auditorium. No questions, no exchange of ideas, no personalities. Still, hardly anyone cut Cheyne's lectures. He was funny. A witty man who never laughed at his own jokes or even cracked a smile. At most there would be an arch expression that let you see he knew he'd said something especially amusing. The first week his students seemed confused by what reaction might be permissible or expected. A few laughed, but a shade too loudly, and with some self-consciousness. A few lectures later, when they realized he expected them to enjoy his sallies, they would be roaring appreciatively. Cheyne would pause only till the laughter had passed its peak and then continue in his dry, studied fashion.

If a student wanted to ask a question when the lecture

had ended, Cheyne would answer politely and to the student's satisfaction, but he would already be clutching his books as if he had no wish to be detained further.

Norman had leaped to the lectern one day, after Cheyne had delivered an enthusiastic review of Renaissance Italian architecture, and loomed so abruptly before him that he saw the professor look startled, almost frightened, and grip his books to his chest defensively. Norman had colored and mumbled something about collateral reading. Cheyne seemed to unfocus his eyes, recited three or four titles and their authors, then sidled quickly past him and out the door.

It was the only time Norman had addressed him in class and he felt clumsy and stupid afterwards. He went to the art library at once and spent over an hour browsing through some texts, till he remembered he was far behind in his other work—work that might help his career if he could stick it out, if he didn't have to think about getting a job, about marrying Marilyn. He piled the books regretfully and carried them back to the desk.

He would marry Marilyn, of course. But he'd finish this semester first. There was still time for that. Even if she would begin to "show" soon, she could sacrifice that much for him, damn it. Let her stay home if it bothered her to be seen, or let them marry quietly now and not worry about setting up house together until January. He would have had three years by then. He needed at least to be able to say, *Yes, I had three years of college.* Surely that wasn't too much to ask.

He had thought of a sports scholarship. He was big, but light on his feet and good at any sport he tried. There weren't too many scholarships available at Minnesota, but he was sure he could qualify. If only he were a better student. But he was already working as hard as he could to keep up a B-minus average, and there was Marilyn, and he knew that any other activity would sink him in his studies.

Three years should be enough to put him over the hump. The fourth year could always be finished at night. Perhaps not right away, of course. And studying at night might mean it would be two or even three more years before he received his bachelor's degree. But it could be done.

Still, here it was almost a year since he dropped out, and he hadn't started night school. Of course not. Not with an infant in the house. Too many responsibilities this first year. Too many to allow study. Or dreams.

He thought of Cheyne's face again at the moment he'd startled him by bounding up so suddenly. Cheyne's lips, almost concealed by a thick beard, had parted and sucked in sharply. His eyes wavered slightly behind their heavy tortoise-shell glasses as if about to search for a convenient exit. He smoothly regained control, however, and even forced the most perfunctory smile imaginable toward Norman to hear his question.

It was a pleasant enough face, Norman reflected; the kind of face that encouraged confidences, that offered security if not warmth, and certainly trust. It was only a warning expression hinted at in his eyes that told you— *no*, almost pleaded with you—not to try to get too close.

Cheyne was a slight man, not very tall, and neither his face nor his body suggested any kind of self-indulgence. All was spare, hard, almost severe, until one noticed how his hair merged with his carefully groomed beard in a rather voluptuous mass of light brown curls, with the first shot of gray apparent only around the chin. The lenses of his glasses enlarged his eyes, increasing the suggestion of a startled forest creature when he turned his gaze on someone unexpectedly. Cheyne's fingers were unusually long and tapered and were almost always clutching a book or pencil or even the lapel of his jacket when he was distracted. Later in the course Norman saw a self-portrait by Egon Schiele and thought at once of Professor Cheyne.

Now the recollection of the slender figure tied to the

bedpost returned vividly to Norman. The glasses were gone and the eyes in death had assumed a curious fixed gaze. When he stood in front of the body, it seemed the eyes focused not on him but through him, caught in some intensely personal vision. Norman had stared at the eyes, almost convinced for an instant that if he looked into them deeply enough he would be able to share the object of their rapt attention. Then he would know.

He recalled Detective Hassler's comment about a body like a fag's, without an ounce of muscle. Cheyne must surely have been forty-five years old, and yet the skin on his body was translucently clear, very pale and almost hairless—the flesh of a young man, and in the surprisingly graceful position the body had been frozen into, with one leg supporting the trunk and the other cocked forward, the effect was startling.

It's all in Hassler's hands now, Norman thought regretfully. His own role in the affair had ended once he'd written his report testifying that he and his partner Officer Martin had answered building superintendent Horace Anderson's call to investigate what could now be presumed to be a homicide. As he wrote the memorandum he was struck by how disparately cool the objective recording of facts seemed in contrast to his own perceptions.

And now what the hell was Hassler going to do about it? If the murderer were a vagrant he could be presumed to be out of town by now. Hassler would probably start by rounding up all the known male hustlers with a record of violence. What then? Would he put out a call for anyone suspicious trying to sell paintings to the local galleries? But which paintings? No, it was certain to remain on the books, Norman decided, as an unsolved homicide, with all Hassler's unsavory speculations ultimately accepted as true because they were the only ones recorded. Disgusting!

But then, where would *he* start if he were conducting

the investigation? Anderson said there were never any visitors that he knew of. That the professor might have been a virtual recluse Norman could accept, but with some reservations. Professor Cheyne seemed nervous and shy, but hardly so antisocial that he wouldn't have some friends. Perhaps since the death of his wife—but no, he couldn't have allowed himself to become that isolated. Norman remembered a student and faculty exhibition of paintings, a biennial event. He'd gone to the opening, and Professor Cheyne had been there too—not exactly a ball of fire, but at least he had attended. There was a painting of his in the show, one that Norman had most admired. Within the predictable range of styles and schools exhibited, Cheyne offered a quiet, modest gouache of a frame house by the water with two children dangling their legs off a ramshackle jetty. The painting was evocative, but its controlled execution suggested the precise traditions of the Bauhaus. Norman much preferred it to the flashier paintings surrounding it, yet it had evidently not been singled out for any of the commendations awarded. Then Norman noticed the date and saw that it was nine years old, executed long before any of the other paintings exhibited. He wondered why he recalled the painting so clearly and decided it was because he had just then developed a keener interest in Cheyne's course, and it was the only painting in the show by anyone he had even a vague connection with.

"Norman?"

The voice shook him abruptly from his meditation. He recognized a young man that had been in a few of his classes.

"Louis."

The young man did not smile and seemed worried. "Norman. Hi. I'm glad you remember me. Listen, you're a cop, aren't you?"

"Yes, I am." He tried not to sound defensive. "And you should be getting your degree pretty soon, right?"

Louis nodded. "I started in the graduate school this semester. Norman, have you heard anything about Professor Cheyne?"

"What?"

"You remember Cheyne. Art department. A kind of thin, middle-aged guy with a beard and glasses. Very quiet, but a good man."

"Yes, I know who you mean all right, but why are you asking?"

"He missed all his classes this week, and then this afternoon someone said he'd been murdered."

Norman scrutinized him. Louis was tall, almost as tall as he, but weighed perhaps twenty pounds less. More a swimmer's body. Or tennis maybe. He was wearing the same punk jeans and work shirt as everyone else under his blue nylon windbreaker, but there was something about the assured way he spoke that told Norman he had money. *He* wouldn't have to drop out of school for the first lousy break to come his way and tie himself down to a wife and kid. He shrugged off the thought and concentrated on what Louis was telling him.

"Nobody'd seen him for a couple of days, and then someone started the story that he was knocked off and now it's all over campus. I thought since you were at the police station you might have heard something about it."

"It's true all right. We found him today. The janitor got suspicious and put in a call."

"How? Why would anyone want to kill him? Him, of all people? Have you found out who did it?"

"Knife wounds. No, not really. He was probably dead before he got—I'm sorry, I don't much want to talk about it if you don't mind. You'll probably hear all about it tomorrow."

"Listen, Norman. Please. I'm not just asking because I need a cheap thrill. He was important to me. I'm an art major and he was—"

Norman sighed. "Can I buy you a cup of coffee?"

"Thanks, but it's on me."

"No. I'm a working man now."

In the coffee shop there was only one customer reading in a far booth. A radio was playing just loudly enough to give them some privacy. Louis searched Norman's face closely for the first time. His impression of Norman at school was that he was not overly bright—another of the school jocks—a little too big, too beefy, someone you spoke to if you'd forgotten your pencil or needed a match. He'd probably pick up a degree in engineering and marry before he got fat.

Now the fact that Norman had left school made him seem suddenly more mature. The tousled blondish hair that had lain long on his shoulders was trimmed to a length more acceptable to the police department, and he looked harder, more formed. His skin didn't seem so florid, and there was a tired but more expressive look to his eyes.

Norman was not particularly handsome. His nose was bulbous and his jaw too prominent, and although he bought his clothes at the same surplus store half the school did, he seemed less concerned about size, invariably choosing the largest size available of anything he bought.

It seemed to Louis that no one still in school had changed as much as Norman had this year. He wondered whether this was an inevitable consequence of going into the outside world. Louis thought he wanted to be a painter, but the idea of pursuing art after graduation didn't seem to him a drastic separation from the University. And, of course, he still entertained the idea of teaching painting or art history, should it become necessary.

They both unzipped their dark blue nylon jackets and hunched over their coffees.

"Did you know Cheyne well?" Norman asked.

"Yeah, I suppose as well as any of his students, for

all that means. I've had a course with him every term for the last two years, but he wasn't someone you could get real close to."

"That's what I hear."

"I tried to get to know him." He shook his head. "He always gave me A's, but he didn't like me."

"Why do you say that?"

Louis shrugged, "He didn't. You'd have to know him to see how he was around students. Not just students—everybody."

"I know. I took his art history."

"Oh, that's just a crap course. He was different in his regular classes—with art majors."

Norman stiffened. "He was very good. Funny."

"Sure, the rock that wisecracks but never cracks. Okay, you told me all the details, but you haven't told me what the cops think. Do they have a suspect? Something to go on?"

"Well, it's murder, of course. Beyond that, there's not much to go on."

Louis didn't attempt to conceal his irritation. "But they must have some theories. How are they following this up? It shouldn't take much to track down his last days. He hasn't had much to do with anyone since his wife died three years ago. He was all alone."

"The detective figures he was gay." Norman felt uncomfortable stating this.

"What?"

"He was tied to the bedpost naked and stabbed. They think he may have picked up a wrong number. There's a lot of weird punks roaming around. Some junkie maybe. A gay guy takes a lot of chances bringing guys home. Jesus."

"No." Louis stiffened.

"What do you mean?"

"I mean you're full of shit. He wasn't gay."

Norman stuttered with embarrassment. "Look, I'm not

the kind who goes around—I mean, it takes all kinds. You can never tell what's going on inside a person's head."

Louis' eyes were burning. "He was *not gay*." A waitress turned to look at them at the sound of his raised voice and quickly went back to mopping Formica with a damp paper napkin.

"Take it easy. You asked me what the police were thinking and I told you. Now if you have any other information about someone—a girl on campus maybe—I think you have a responsibility to tell me about it. I'll try to keep your name out of it if I can, but you have a—"

"Fuck you." Louis rose, threw a dollar on the counter and hurried out.

"Hey!" Norman half-rose, then abruptly sat down again and stared into his coffee, shielding his eyes with his hands. He forced himself to finish the coffee and wait a few minutes. Before leaving he went to the phone and spoke into it quite loudly. "Marilyn? Honey, I'll be home in just a few minutes. No, I had to see an old buddy who's having some problems. Has the kid eaten yet? Okay, I'll be right there."

He pointedly said good night to the waitress, who fluted an answer without turning from the box of spoons she was replenishing. A light snowfall had started, the season's first, and Norman drew his neck into the collar of his flight jacket and hunched into the wind. "If anybody's a fag," he thought, "it's got to be Louis. Why are they so damn touchy? Who gives a shit anyway!" He decided to splurge and hailed a taxi.

LOUIS

Louis drove up to a faultlessly restored townhouse halfway up a hill that offered an almost unobstructed view of the lake. The brass finials on the black wrought-iron fence were kept highly polished, and the plantings in the redwood boxes were changed four times a year and trimmed weekly, winter and summer. The landscapers had been there that afternoon, but Louis paused only briefly to glance at the bittersweet and dwarf pine that had begun to trap the first flakes of snow on their branches. The chrysanthemums were still beautiful this morning, he thought. What did they do with them?

Heap was standing in the entrance hall, her legs firmly parted for balance as she greeted him.

"Ho. Beauty returns. I thought you were going to come home early and paint, or I'd have straightened out your studio for you."

"Thanks. I told you not to bother. I can never find anything when you've been in there."

She held out her cheek for a peck. "You're a wretch but I still love you. I'll have your tini in a mini. All ready in the fridge."

She took his jacket and shook it out before hanging it in the closet.

"Heap, I'm going to my room. I want a tub. Are you alone?"

She tossed her head and announced theatrically, "We are always alone, but there's no one here if that's what you mean. And after I bring you your tini I'm going to take my headache to bed. Dinner's in the warming oven any time you want it." She weaved unsteadily toward the kitchen.

Louis stripped off his clothes at once and picked up a copy of *Art News* while he waited for the tub to fill. He threw the quilted blue and gold silk spread off the bed and stretched out. How he despised the decor of this room. The Napoleon Room—but it had been this way long before he moved in three years ago, and the amenities were certainly superior to those offered by the Y.

The carved posts had medallions of Napoleon's profile halfway up, and swags of gold and blue flounced from the baldequin. The tables were cluttered with eagles and bees, and the walls were hung with gilt-edged prints of ladies in Empire bodices, except for a space over the headboard that was given over to a smoky oil of a water battle.

"Still not a goddamn decent reading light in this room." Heap came in without knocking, carrying a small silver tray with two crystal brandy snifters. "You don't mind your tini in these, do you darling? Much less chance of spilling any and I don't have to run my ass off for refills."

She wore an ankle-length floral printed kaftan that suited her tall, angular body, and her strawberry-colored hair was cut short and shaped closely to her head.

"Heap, do you think I could put a larger light bulb, maybe a flood, in this stupid little lamp?"

"Forget it. You already asked that once. I thought I'd have a drink with you to keep you company. Let me go see how your bath's coming." She stepped into the bathroom and returned with her arm wet to the elbow. "It's fine. Come on in and bring your drink and I'll scrub your back."

"No thanks. I just want to relax in it if you don't mind. No soap. Just a nice, long soak. I'm tense as a cat tonight. I nearly totalled the Porsche going down Sixth Street."

"Trouble is, you drink too much coffee during the day, dear. Now finish your drink and I'll fetch us another. There's a whole jar in the freezer."

"I've had a lot to think about today. Not a good day at all. Okay, let me go soak." She patted his ass playfully with her wet hand as he passed by.

"Heap, may I ask a personal question?"

"I have no secrets from you, Beauty."

"I mean very personal. About your husband." The water came right up to the top of his neck and felt marvelous.

"That's not personal. That's ancient history."

"When he died, did you ever think of marrying again?"

"Nope."

"Because you still loved him?"

"Nope."

"But I'm sure lots of men wanted to marry you."

"Of course. I was gorgeous. Pooh! All widows get lots of offers."

"Were you depressed for a long time?"

"Nope."

He rubbed the back of his neck with a wet sponge.

"Never mind my dumb questions."

"I don't. And although you didn't ask, if you were wondering if I ever had another lover, the answer is still nope. Let me fill your glass and then I'll go to my room. I want to finish my book and take a nap so I can wake up for the late, late movie. Joan Crawford *and* Bette Davis tonight at 2:30."

She returned with a pitcher and set it on the tray. "I'll leave the rest here for you. There's not much left. Maybe I'll mix another batch and put them in the freezer before I go to bed, just in case."

"I'm fine, but go ahead."

She leaned over the tub and brushed his lips with her

mouth. "Goodnight, Beauty. Try and get some sleep tonight. You look all in."

"Goodnight, Heap."

She staggered out of the room, carefully closing the door behind her.

Louis pressed his eyelids shut and let his body slide deeper in the tub. Professor Cheyne's face, sad, almost reproachful, confronted him at once—as he had been sure it would.

When did the whole messy business start? Cheyne was a familiar figure to him almost as soon as he started at the University. If you were interested in painting, he was one important reason why you chose the University of Minnesota. For a long time Louis had no reason to believe he was any more to Cheyne than another face in the sea of faces that confronted him in every class.

A few months ago, only toward the end of the semester before last, Louis was surprised by an unexpected overture. On the opening day of the student-faculty art biennial, Louis had been greeted by the secretary of the art department as soon as he entered the exhibition.

"Professor Cheyne wants to see you." She jerked her thumb toward a corner where Cheyne was standing, nibbling a pretzel stick and forcing a smile to his lips whenever someone came close.

"Professor Cheyne?"

He swallowed the last inch of pretzel and sprang forward to seize another from the bowl nearby. "Yes?"

"You wanted to see me?"

"I did?"

"I'm Louis Denoyer. Miss Thwaites said—"

"Oh yes, yes. Oh, I believe you're a student of mine, aren't you?"

"I am." Louis furrowed his brow. Didn't even remember him, and the class was already four weeks old. There had been a lecture series the term before, too.

"I wanted to ask you something about your painting."

"I haven't seen it yet. Where did they hang it?"

The Professor moved quickly out of his corner. "It's here, in this other room. A little crowded, but the light's good on it."

Louis felt Professor Cheyne studying him keenly. Did he always look so disapproving? There was something disquieting about his cool appraisal and Louis suddenly wished he hadn't dressed so smartly that morning. Cheyne clearly disapproved of the color of his shirt. "You don't mind if I go with you, do you? I'd like another look, and I'd also like to speak to you about it."

"Thanks." Louis wondered if he always spoke this stiffly.

"I find I like the painting very much."

"Thank you."

The professor scanned him again. "You must be about twenty."

"Twenty-one. I started painting seriously a little over two years ago."

"Do you have good space, with quiet, to work in at home?"

Louis blushed fiercely. "Yes." A hint of annoyance crept into his voice and he covered it quickly. "I have a studio set up and I try to work every day."

"You must. I take it, then, that you are serious about becoming a painter?"

"I am a painter."

"No, so far you are simply painting. And very well. I certainly don't mean to belittle you, but becoming a painter is much more special."

"Oh?"

"You have to decide it's so important that nothing else matters very much. It isn't easy. You're very young and must have many interests. Interests can be distractions. What I'm asking is—and I'm afraid I shall phrase it in a way that will sound quaint to you—will you make painting your mistress?"

It was Louis' turn to stare. "I think of myself as serious," he answered coolly.

"Then let me help you."

"You have. I've already learned a great deal from you. What about you, Professor? Do you paint?"

"Yes—that is, I used to. Lately—"

"Do you have something here?"

"Across from yours."

Louis walked directly to Cheyne's painting and studied it a moment. "It's not what I would have expected from you. I mean, you're very good of course." He glanced at the date. "How come you wanted to show this one?"

"Please. Never mind. I'm glad you saw it, so that you'll know that I do know something about painting beyond theory. But painting just isn't the same for me anymore. I once wanted to make it my life. I had a passion. Yes, a passion, but one that wouldn't be satisfied. Not by me. I couldn't be true to it. Oh, what nonsense I'm talking. But I believe *you* could become a painter. A master. I know you're good now, but I hope you're not satisfied. You could become—"

"What?"

"Everything a painter should be."

"I feel silly saying thanks all the time. I think I know what you're trying to tell me. Look, I'm not afraid of hard work." He was tempted to say, "If you paid more attention to what I've been doing in class you'd see that."

"Do you have direction?"

Louis looked puzzled. "Sure."

"We'll be able to understand each other more later. I'm glad you're in my class. Which class is it? 'Color?'"

"No," he answered irritably. "I'll take that next term. I'm in 'The Artist and His Materials.'"

"Good. Half workshop, half classroom. You can get anything you wish out of that course if you let me show you how."

"Professor—how come?"

"I beg your pardon?"

"How come? There's lots of guys that are pretty good.

Lo Bianco's doing fine work, and Simpson too. Why are you hitting on me?"

The Professor looked puzzled, and then embarrassed. "I'm afraid I—"

"Or put it another way—what's in it for you?"

Cheyne stared at him a moment. "I thought I recognized an exceptional talent, but I've been wrong before." He sighed and then stiffened. "I promise you that if I am wrong I will give you no cause to regret my interest. Good day, Louis."

Louis soaked his sponge and held it over his head, squeezing rivulets of lukewarm water down his face. *God, what a fool I am.*

Work assignments in class became increasingly difficult from that day on. When the summer session arrived, Louis assumed that classes would be more relaxed and that Cheyne might let up a bit, but the pressure on him became stronger. However much harder Cheyne drove him, there was never any praise, certainly never flattery, only just enough encouragement to keep him working. When Louis asked him once to join him for a coffee between classes, he refused.

Louis asked Cheyne on another occasion to accompany him on a walk after class one day when he had awakened to a whole new area in his work that he hesitated to explore before discussing it with Cheyne. The professor walked no more than a hundred yards with him, answered his questions, and then excused himself abruptly and left.

It was inevitable that Cheyne's attitude toward him in class should begin to alter perceptibly. Other students recognized that Louis had a stronger drive and highly developed gifts, so it did not seem extraordinary that Cheyne would pay more attention to him. And Cheyne's ironclad approach could hardly inspire envy of his favored student. But after months of guiding him, now that Louis was in the color class, Cheyne began to grow increasingly distracted. Sometimes he would break off in the middle of a sentence, and then the class would follow his gaze to Louis. It was an uncompromising stare, but Louis had begun to feel embarrassed by it. He left his customary seat toward the front of the class and began to sit in the last row, well behind the other students. Cheyne never commented on this and continued his classes with his customary equanimity, but he grew increasingly demanding of the efforts he drew from Louis, and Louis had long since stopped feeling flattered by his expectations.

One day, right after the fall session had begun, Louis cut a class for the first time since Cheyne had undertaken his tutelage. They passed each other on the way to class two days later and Louis greeted him cheerfully without offering a word of excuse. It was a warm day, one of the last of early fall, and Louis wore a pair of tight white jeans and a stretch-knit T-shirt. Louis grinned when he saw Cheyne color slightly as he looked up and down at his costume. He took his customary seat at the rear of the class, and it seemed that Cheyne was very careful to avoid looking his way. The young man was amused at first, and then exultant. It looked like they might be playing a game whose rules he understood, and one in which his experience led him to believe he would soon gain the uncontested upper hand. He interrupted Cheyne to ask a question, not an especially pertinent one, and his tone was unusually lighthearted. But Cheyne's answer was abrupt, almost reproachful.

The next day in class he wore his usual blue jeans, but he let one leg stretch out into the aisle and kept his left hand casually placed on his crotch. When Cheyne glanced at him, he saw the professor color slightly again, but only for an instant, and then he avoided looking at him for the rest of the session. When class ended, Louis went up to the front desk as he customarily did to speak to the professor, but this time he carefully pressed his body forward against the top of the desk, allowing the surface edge to press just below his crotch and throw his genitals into relief.

Cheyne was cool. "Louis," he said, "it's easy to be led astray when you are young."

His voice was tight and Louis saw clearly how exhausted Cheyne seemed. The summer sun had never touched him and his eyes had hollowed.

"I don't understand, Professor."

"Perhaps you don't. I was referring, of course, to the class you cut earlier this week. I suggest you fight very hard right now to keep your sights on your goals."

"Professor, I've never worked as hard as I have this month, and you should know it."

"Good. I intend to give you an opportunity at once to demonstrate it. Will you please bring me some of your work, the things you do at your studio; sketches, studies—anything, I don't care."

"Okay. My place or yours?" he answered, smirking.

Professor Cheyne remained unflustered. " I have a free period after Friday's class. Bring them then and I promise to give them my full attention."

He stared a long time into Louis' face, an undecipherable stare that would have to open into something else before any hint of meaning could be revealed. Louis yielded first and lowered his eyes.

At the next class meeting Louis wore his tight white jeans again and stretched his leg down the aisle. His hand lay along his crotch, somewhat carelessly, but he could rub himself with the back of his hand, quite subtly, until he was half-erect.

Cheyne glanced at him coolly once or twice after the first few minutes of this, but if he noticed anything, it was difficult to tell. Louis thought he looked less well than usual today, as if he were fighting off a migraine, but now that he'd gone this far he was too excited by his sport to stop it. He waited a long time for Cheyne to look his way again, then laced his hands behind his head and arched his back, thrusting his groin with its enlarged organ forward while he pretended to yawn.

Cheyne's eyes lingered on him a moment, but his reaction was to pause in his lecture while he clenched his jaws—tight enough, it seemed, to make his eyes water, as if the migraine had suddenly become worse.

At the end of class, Louis went up to his desk again and they waited till the rest of the students had left. Cheyne looked intently at him, his voice fully controlled.

"I don't like your games. They're cheap."

"Why, Professor, I don't understand. If I were to play games with you, I don't think they'd be cheap." The cunning in his eyes betrayed the mock innocence of his voice.

Cheyne raised his hand deliberately and struck the boy a sharp blow across the mouth. "Don't forget to bring me your work tomorrow."

Louis recoiled, but he saw that tears had formed in Cheyne's eyes. He stood silently until the professor was out of the room, then brought a handkerchief to his face and inspected the tiny drop of blood his lip had left on it.

Louis stood in the tub and turned the cold shower on until he was jolted out of his reverie. *Less than a week ago. I never even had the time to straighten it out with him. If only I could have told him—what? That I was just having fun? That I was sorry?*

He stepped cautiously from the tub and, without drying himself, drained the rest of the martinis from the pitcher Heap had left. He started back to get a towel when the door opened and a tall man in his mid-fifties entered.

"Hi, baby." He walked over and pressed a full kiss on Louis' mouth. "Jesus, dry yourself. That rug'll be ruined if you do that. It's very old, baby. If you let it get wet you might rot the fibers." He walked into the bathroom and threw Louis a towel. "You look like you've had more than your usual. Didn't you get any work done today?"

"No, Bill. I've had a really rough day."

"Well, you look it. Is Heap in bed?"

"Yes."

He grimaced. "Well, I didn't feel like eating her crap anyway. Why don't we call the girls and see if they'd like to go for a lobster? And don't try to work anymore tonight. You've been overdoing it. It's hard to get rid of those shadows under the eyes once they start. You're getting washed out!"

"Bill. Come here, please." Louis put his arms around his lover's neck. "Bill, Bill! Cheyne is dead. Murdered." He shook his head numbly.

"What!" Bill pulled himself free. "How? Who?"

"No one knows. If he were gay they'd have a good story. He was tied up to the bedpost naked and stabbed."

"Not gay, huh? Who are you trying to kid? Do you think I don't know what's been going on between you two?" He pushed Louis away, but not roughly. "What do you take me for?"

Louis shook his head. "Bill, I don't say there might not have been something if he were for it. I got silly and played a crummy little cockteasing game with him. Not serious, you know. Oh, I suppose I just wanted to get to him, break him down a little. But there was nothing there."

"You're a bitch." Bill sank to the bed and sat there a moment before speaking again. "Get your clothes on. I'll call the girls."

"Bill, I suppose I shouldn't have told you. I'm sorry."

"Don't give it a thought. When you get tired of me, you always know what you can do. You might even be able to get your old room back at the Y. Now hurry up and get dressed." He paused a moment and his voice turned even more acid. "By the way, I don't suppose it could ever have occurred to you—"

"What?"

"That you just weren't his type."

Louis sat on the bed next to Bill and reached for his hand, but Bill made no move to extend it toward him. "I think Heap said there were more drinks in the fridge. I'll go get us some. Okay, Bill? Okay?"

ELISSA

There was absolutely nothing wrong with that painting, he decided. Professor Cheyne glanced briefly at some others nearby from the brushes of two of his colleagues in the art department and decided they couldn't hold up under scrutiny in another ten years without appearing, well, shallow. The best thing he could say for them was that they were fashionable, a word he reserved as a substitute for contemptible. Even the paintings in the show that looked the most honest he saw as derived pretty unimaginatively from their betters of the thirties and forties. There were two neo-Feiningers and four neo-Klees. At least they reflected taste, he thought. The two neo-Pollacks he didn't even glance at. You could always spot a genuine Pollack in a roomful of his imitators no matter how similar they might appear to the uninitiated. He bemoaned again the hermetic turn that art had assumed, making it such a target for the critics who should know better but didn't. When a clever man like Tom Wolfe could make such an ass of himself, what could one expect from the well-meaning but uneducated? He interrupted his train of thought lest it lead him into what he identified as the sinister trap of elitism.

But look at the hyper-realists who walked off with all the honors this year! They were, ultimately, absurd. The technique was so transparent, and he felt any competent draughtsman could be taught to do as well in a short time. A photo enlarger, an airbrush. Ah, much better to leave that to the art directors in advertising agencies. As a technician, he was certainly superior to these efforts, and he knew he had another quality that was missing in these giant, vacuous canvasses. Taste.

Did it count for nothing anymore? What was there in these street scenes that Hopper hadn't done definitively years ago? And all that flashy concentration on reflective surfaces! The Flemish schools handled it so much better. Even movie directors—who was it? Stanley Donen had virtually exhausted it as a source of visual interest.

The only painting he felt he needed to go back to for a second look, and then a third, was by someone whose name he couldn't place. Denoyer. Not an art department instructor. But who else could have that fine a command of his materials? No one of the students working on a master's degree. He knew that crowd of louts by name, and all too well. He'd been fooled once before six years ago by a fine painting somewhat reminiscent of Kenneth Noland that turned out to be by a young instructor in mathematics who stayed only one year and then made an auspicious marriage and moved to the Seychelles—where, Professor Cheyne decided, he might continue to pursue his art advantageously, provided he didn't mind working in a cultural vacuum (often a capital idea) and could have adequate supplies shipped in from the mainland.

He would have to ask Miss Thwaites who this Denoyer person was. The painting had been signed in a small but absolutely legible hand, rather remarkable amid the vanity of personal imprints on the others.

The painting was ostensibly representational, which aroused no prejudice one way or the other in Cheyne, who sought only what his skilled eye recognized as painterly qualities. The canvas had been divided into three horizontal bands indicating sky, earth, and subsoil. The subsoil held a fantastic complex of roots and rhizomes, tunnels and cunning strata populated by underground creatures. The central band was a modest landscape translated into a geometric interlacing of tree trunks and foliage half-concealing a world of timid fauna. At the top, the canvas was expanded into a vast skyscape, with the tops of the trees piercing the openness of an infinity punctuated by the presence of an occasional bird. The color transitions within the three bands fascinated the professor. He knew no one at the University who could have handled it as well, yet it had not been singled out for any honorable mention. Something in the draughtsmanship suggested a *naif*, but the details were too cleverly organized to have been developed by anyone except a gifted and well-practiced painter.

It was almost a shock when Denoyer presented himself. Somehow Cheyne was expecting someone totally different, a more interior person with a more modest appearance. For the work to be the product of this rather aggressive and very worldly-looking young man—oh no, he looked like he'd be more at home with a surfboard than a paintbrush. And those eyes. Deep blue and with a pleasant, open quality, but they too told you he was accustomed to getting anything he wanted. Yes, this was a person who knew all the shortcuts, and Cheyne knew there were no shortcuts to the goals he set. How could this whelp, this fugitive from American International Pictures be the artist who—well, we'd see.

Professor Cheyne's mind was busily devising one certain way to check the young man's motivations. The first time they were assured of a weekend of perfect weather, he would hand him an assignment that would soon tell whether he was a worker or couldn't resist the chance to spend a precious weekend stretching that splendid body out in the sun somewhere to be admired and—never mind that, he thought crossly.

The following Friday he handed Louis a typewritten sheet. Louis glanced at it and flushed.

"When would you like this?"

"Monday, of course. You should be able to work out at least one interesting solution by then. More if you find it stimulating. Tempera should be fine, but suit yourself. You may want to play around with some other media as well. Some nice transparent watercolor washes might be

fun. But remember, stick to what I've laid down. It's only
by observing the restrictions within a given problem that
the artist can display his freedom."

Louis was still staring at the sheet when Cheyne left
him. Not until the third reading did he grasp what his
weekend would involve. The assignment was headed:

A COLOR EXPERIENCE FOR LOUIS DENOYER
An extension of Value, Intensity, and Temperature into
a working color experience.

a) A juxtaposition of temperature contrasts within
one color family, warm to conflict with cool, both at
exactly the same value.

b) An attempt to strengthen the intensity of these
color states by contrast with less intense or grayer areas
of color.

THE COLOR STRUCTURE

1) Choose a pair of temperature opposites in the same
family; e.g., blue-green and yellow-green or yellow-or-
ange and yellow-green. Select another pair of opposites
that includes one of the preceding pair; e.g., blue-green
and blue-violet.

2) Each pair is rendered at approximately the middle
value; however, the values of both should be the same. (If
BG and YG are used, add white to the former mixture to
bring it to the value state of YG.)

3) Remember that opaque watercolor dries lighter in
value than the wet mixture. In testing for identical values
make color swatches of both and compare the dried states.

4) We have, then, opposites in temperature of a relatively strong intensity at visually the same value. Now, by
a particular color-surround we attempt to present these
intensities as still stronger ones.

THE FORMAL STRUCTURE

1) Select a geometric shape or a variation thereof; e.g.,
an "almost" rectangle, one whose edges are not quite
parallel. Align two forms of this shape side by side so that
common edges touch. Permit one shape to penetrate the
other on this common edge. One shape is the cool color
member, the other the warm; e.g., BG and YG.

2) Repeat this pairing of shapes in another part of the visual field. One of the above colors appears in this new pairing (e.g., BG) to be accompanied by a new temperature juxtaposition (e.g., BV). We are thus working with BG/YG and BG/BV, or BG/YG and YG/YO.

3) Surround both pairs with several layers of shapes as the flesh of an avocado surrounds the seed. Vary the widths or sizes of these layers. Eventually layers surrounding one pair of shapes will merge with those surrounding the second.

THE FUSION OF COLOR AND FORM

1) The layers relating to one shape will be grayer, less intense variations of the color of that shape. They become increasingly grayer as they move outward from that shape. The graying medium may be black, or the complement, or both. If BG is repeated in both sets of pairs, one shape might be surrounded by BG grayed with RO, the other surrounded by BG grayed with black.

2) If a yellow is grayed with either violet or black it becomes darker. The same darkening by graying occurs with orange, as the complement is darker. In color, treat the layer-surround in these two ways:

a) The layers surrounding one color become increasingly darker as they become grayer.

b) The layers become grayer as they move out from the shape but retain the same value as the inside shape. Note: There are four shapes that can be treated as suggested above.

SUMMATION

a) There will be two areas of strong intensity. Consider the placement of these in relation to the visual whole.

b) There will be areas of darker value. Consider the distribution of these. Be alert to the placement of lighter values—those areas that are grayer than the color-shape but identical in value.

c) Consider the color-merging of the outer layers of one unit with those of the other.

Louis, it might be best if you approach the execution first as an academic problem, and then once you have satisfactorily illustrated the phenomena set out, you might incorporate them all in a painting, perhaps a landscape. Have an enjoyable weekend.   E.C.

Professor Cheyne walked to the art library but stopped off first at an adjoining lounge reserved for the faculty and lighted a cigarette. What a cruel afternoon. The gall of Dean Whitcomb, that ass who understood nothing of painting, who couldn't be trusted to know a Mondrian from a Fragonard, to suggest to him that at future art faculty shows he would do better to show something more contemporary. More contemporary! The idiot meant more recent, of course. But then what could you expect from a man who allowed his wife to decorate their living room with Yugoslav *naifs*, picked up, no doubt, on an ill-advised vacation. Cheyne had once attended a faculty tea (martinis or white wine) at their residence, almost at gunpoint, that had left him insomniac for two nights after. There was a pseudo-Early American living room with the Yugoslav *naifs*, a French Provincial dining room curtained and wallpapered in the wrong pink *Toile de Jouy*, pronounced by the hostess, with no conscious attempt at humor, as "toile de juif"; and then the hidden parts of the house to which he declined after the offer of a tour of inspection, certain they were outfitted in Mother Goose Gothic.

It was an impertinence, no less, to criticize his work. Didn't his courses attract students from all over the country, and weren't his peers unanimously respectful? There wasn't a color course to compare with his, now that Albers had died. Could this upstart dean's ultimatum be the equivalent of "publish or perish?" What an appalling idea!

How could he concentrate now on his own painting? During the first years of teaching he begrudged every hour that his classes kept him from his studio. They had lived in the country then, an hour's drive from the University, and Elissa would drive him in every morning because she felt his work kept him too distracted to drive well. They had a fine stone farmhouse with a Normandy barn that he used for his work. His days there were often interrupted only by meals, or when he allowed himself to be cajoled away by Elissa for some entertainment she had organized.

It was Elissa who announced to him in the mornings that they were going to the theater that evening or having friends in to dinner, she who bought the concert or ballet tickets and planned their vacations (a new European country every other year, the mountains in between). She ran every part of their lives that wasn't directly involved with his painting or teaching. And she did it effortlessly. There was an old Swedish woman to help around the house, but the imaginative dishes that appeared at the table were all Elissa's.

Their garden was a joy. Crocuses and snowdrops pushed through the snow to herald the end of winter, and chrysanthemums held their bronze heads high till long after neighboring gardens had yielded to the cold. Elissa's peonies and Christmas cactus were famous, and she had to leave him two or three times a month to address garden clubs all over the midwest.

These recollections were far from painful to Cheyne. He was fortunate enough to have secured his favorite chair in the lounge today, so he lighted another cigarette and allowed himself the indulgence of continuing his reverie without another thought of Dean Whitcomb.

Elissa had been a marvelous weaver. Her work was in some of the most distinguished collections in the country, yet the fabrics she used in their home were varied and eclectic. There were simple yet sumptuous Peruvian fabrics used in clever juxtaposition to her own in the living room, and the counterpanes in the bedrooms ranged from the products of sixteenth-century Irish convents to the work of West Virginia farmwomen.

He needed to comfort himself by asking and answering again the question that posed itself so often. Did she resent his dependence on her? Probably not. After all, there were no children. And did *he* resent that same dependence? No, not even when he missed it so desperately now. Then why—

He used to enjoy sexual relations with her so intensely. They both appeared to be satisfied. Cheyne thought of himself as a lusty man then. But it was Elissa who prepared the way, and now that she was gone he had simply stopped. Odd how simple it was. It might just as effectively have dropped off for all the care it gave him now.

A year after her death, when he was still entertained socially on occasion (the invitations soon dwindled rapidly), he was engaged in a pleasant discussion with a faculty wife when it occurred to him quite abruptly that she was flirting—actively leaving herself open for seduction. He found the notion appalling and left her side before they had quite finished their conversation. Later that evening he allowed himself to be amused by his reaction, which he admitted was somewhat more appropriate to one of the Brontë sisters' declining an invitation to a drive-in.

Things simply didn't work anymore. He sold the farmhouse, or rather his lawyer did. The offer seemed generous enough. Of course, it included all furnishings and art objects. But why not? Painting no longer interested him and he preferred not to live surrounded by the accumulations of their shared years. The new owners permitted him to take with him the painting of his childhood home by the jetty, and a length of striped fabric that Elissa had been working on. He moved at once into a conveniently located apartment whose availability had been advertised on the University bulletin board. He doubted that Elissa would have liked it much, but it offered more room that it seemed to him he could possibly need.

Elissa. She had been named for Elissa Landi, the fairest patrician of Hollywood's Golden Age, and although there was no blood tie to her namesake, she had a distinguishing blonde grace and delicate manners. Children were not possible for them, but it didn't matter much to Cheyne. It would take a lengthy and painful operation to right a perverse displacement of her organs and it didn't seem worth it. Elissa became his child and his parents as well as his mate. He was sorry he couldn't allow a dog or a cat into the house to keep her company, but his allergies wouldn't permit it. Even the proximity of a neighbor's hamster made his eyes swell. Still, there was not a more cheerful wife he knew and he counted his blessings.

Cheyne crushed out his cigarette savagely. It had been so beautiful for him. If it wasn't as easy for her, why had she never said so? She had never once complained, never found him wanting as a husband, a provider, or a lover. A lover! He was certain she'd never wanted another.

Why then? What depraved, interior devil had urged her one night to end her life? No muss, no fuss. Just the empty bottle and a simple note. "Take care of yourself, Elliott. I'm so damned tired. Love. Elissa." What kind of grotesque joke was that?

There was a fair sum of money disposed of in her will. The house and furnishings were Cheyne's. It had tacitly been understood that they would live on what he earned. The only luxury that Elissa had ever bought and paid for with her own money was a greenhouse attached to the rear of the house with an elaborate system for temperature and humidity control, a "Gro-lux" wing for seedlings and ailing plants that turned out to be a hospital where the neighbors would send their enfeebled specimens for her to nurse back to health. Cheyne was shocked to learn that this project had cost over $30,000 but was pleased that she could indulge herself.

Elissa's will was explicit. Cheyne, she was certain, would have no idea what to do with a large sum of money, so her estate was left, virtually *in toto*, to various orphanages and organizations for the care of destitute children. Cheyne was touched, and actually delighted. How like her.

But she had wronged him utterly by taking her life. He saw no malice in it. She couldn't have known she was condemning him to a half-life, but it was hard not to resent what he came to think of as the only truly selfish act of her life. She expected him to marry again. At least she'd said so on the occasions when, curled up in bed together, they had woolgathered aloud as lovers do and made each other swear that if anything happened to the other, etc., etc. Hardly the sort of talk one takes seriously after breakfast. Still, the thought of a liaison with another woman was unthinkable, almost shocking.

One didn't expose oneself to a stranger, and after Elissa, all other women were essentially foreign. But he was aware that he would have to allow himself to be more socially engaged again. He was becoming strange and he knew it. It was time to fight. Involvement. He'd taken the first step, he assured himself. Hadn't he taken on a protegé of sorts? He didn't feel entirely convinced of his judgment where Louis was concerned, but surely it was a step in the right direction. Now it was time to start thinking about his own career. He had tenure, and his reputation as a teacher seemed secure, but it wouldn't do to remain still. That's probably what Dean Whitcomb was hinting. In a sense, he supposed, the stuffy bastard was right. If he were to reenter life more fully, it would not be enough to attempt to do so vicariously through the accomplishments of a student who was, after all, nothing to him. No, nothing. He wished he could like the young man more, but his prejudice against—against what? His good looks? Well, they weren't the sort of good looks he admired, but he would try to be more fair.

He would paint again. The idea had occurred to him with increasing frequency over the last two weeks, but it was so hard to take up again from where he had left off. The dining room of his apartment was never used and would make an excellent studio. The table could be resurfaced with something more functional, and there was plenty of room for an easel. The chest for linens would do nicely to hold his tools, and the light was excellent. It was simply a new approach to his painting that he needed. Something to demonstrate his draughtsmanship, his ability to control the performance of color, and something else. Wit. How amusing if he could go the hyper-realists one better—beat them at their own game and dazzle them with his superior handling of color.

Perhaps if he were to recreate classic paintings, with painstaking attention to detail and to the style of the master—but alter the color scheme in a way that only an accomplished painter could appreciate. The color key could be reorganized to accentuate formal relationships between values; the shapes modified but never abstracted, to heighten structural relationships. The figures need never be altered and the composition manipulated only very subtly, but oh, what he could do with clothing, backgrounds, and details.

He put out his cigarette and walked into the library with a livelier step than he'd shown in quite a while.

Why not start with a Giorgione? He'd do his best to indicate the reverence he felt for the very finest, but what a triumph if he could play his clever games with an absolutely flawless masterpiece.

The art library had thousands of slides, most of them requisitioned by him for his art history course. He was proud of the extent of the collection. He'd buy a slide projector and some canvas and supplies that afternoon. Should he work in oils? Maybe, but they might take too long to dry, and he detested the smell. Acrylics? Well, the range of colors left much to be desired, but he could manipulate them as well as anyone, and with a decent glaze—no problem there. Now to choose a slide. Giorgione's *Virgin and St. Anne?* He found it awesomely beautiful. Did he dare? The open sweetness of the Virgin's face suggested Elissa to him. A bit more shadow around the cheekbones, the shape of the eyes a little more—yes, it was very like Elissa. He pocketed the slide and hurried to the art supply shop.

It was painstaking work, but Cheyne had time to spare. Barely ten days after he had first projected the Giorgione onto his raw canvas and begun to sketch in the outline in charcoal, he was adding the final tones and giving expression to the delicate nuances with a fine sable brush that held no more than a dozen hairs. He had pored over the painting for hours on end every evening and through the night but had not yet dared to question what he had accomplished with it. Now that he was forced to admit that his art could carry it no further, he dreaded a critical examination. And who, besides himself, was qualified to evaluate what he had attempted? He never cultivated other artists, and his relationship with faculty members was merely polite.

He swallowed the liquid fear that rose in his craw and moved the painting farther from the work light where it could be judged more evenly, but he still avoided evaluating its overall effect. He washed his brushes meticulously, scrubbed the work table by his easel, and then undressed. He took a long, warm shower, fastidiously scrubbing the vestiges of pigment that remained obstinately imbedded under his nails.

Refreshed, he entered his workroom, but he was dissatisfied with the glare of the studio light and moved the painting to the more neutral illumination of the living room. He took down a mirror and hung the painting in its place, then eased himself into the brown corduroy lounge chair where he usually read before retiring and allowed himself to study the picture. He strained to grasp what its initial impact might be on someone viewing it for the first time, and he also tried to dissect it critically, as if he were judging a candidate's entry in a very important show.

There could be no quarrel with his distribution of lights and darks; the composition was perhaps a trifle more obvious after the few changes he had incorporated, but his draughtsmanship was certainly faultless. He looked at it for about half an hour and then went into the studio and extracted a large manila folder from behind the dresser. He took from it the most recent work Louis Denoyer had submitted to him, the solution to the lengthy and perhaps deliberately overexacting assignment he had given him over a week ago. He took some masking tape and attached Denoyer's work to the wall about two feet away from his *Virgin and St. Anne.*

Louis' composition almost danced with vigor, and the colors lay quietly composed but enriched each other harmoniously. There was a new meaning every time he scanned the modest rectangle of rough paper. He took it down ruefully and placed it back in its folder. He would have to write a critique for it later this week. Louis had been asking about it.

He's very good, Cheyne admitted, and then he consoled himself with—*but he's also my creature. He couldn't possibly have done that even a month ago.*

He returned to stare at the neo-Giorgione. He would glaze it tonight or tomorrow, he thought, although he'd used a fairly glossy medium to extend his pigment. The light. It still didn't bring out what he hoped it might. He brought in his studio work light and turned it toward the painting.

It had been a mistake. He should never have substituted Elissa's face for the Virgin's. His hands felt clammy and he had to steady himself a moment. Was it a religious sacrilege or merely a sacrilege because of the reverence he felt towards Giorgione? Nonsense, he scoffed: the models who were used to pose for madonnas and saints were often prostitutes. Elissa might easily be the most virtuous woman ever to have offered her face as a likeness for the Virgin. But why even think about such absurd trifles? He looked at the features again and realized that he had no photographs of Elissa. He disliked cameras, and when Elissa chanced to receive a photograph of herself, she was likely to hold on to it for a while and then discard it during one of her rigorous housecleaning drives.

It was the first time since her death that he'd seen her likeness except in his own imagination. A younger, exquisite Elissa, but it was certainly she. He'd captured every feature he'd loved. But oddly, the calmness in the original Virgin's face was translated into what might be interpreted as sullenness in Elissa's features. The ethereal quality of the expression in Giorgione's Madonna was now merely vacuous. And there was something else he surely hadn't noticed while he was limning her features. Elissa looked slightly annoyed. He tilted the shade of the light downward and looked again. A shadow crossed the face now and she looked almost reproving. He turned the light back up again and lighted a cigarette.

Five minutes later the cigarette stub had burned his fingers and the ash had spotted his naked thigh. He snuffed it out impatiently and tried to brush the soot from his leg but it smeared damply on his skin.

He leaned back in the chair once again and allowed his gaze to remain fixed on the painting until his peripheral vision was blotted out and the painting seemed to fill the entire wall. He sat there until the light coming through the windows startled him into the realization that he'd lost another night's sleep. When had he really slept this week? An hour or two with a book in his lap in this same chair? A few fretful hours in that large, unfriendly bed? He rose reluctantly and realized that he was sopping wet. His seat on the easy chair was stained almost black with moisture. He returned somewhat crossly to the shower, rinsed quickly, and came back into the room mopping himself with an already damp towel.

She was frowning! Was it possible? His hands were trembling as he took the painting down and carried it to the light from the window. The colors appeared chalky and grayed. He reasoned that this was a very cold dawn light, very different from the warm incandescence of the light he painted by. But could he have lost his key so completely? He looked about helplessly, and then with an irrational panic, as if he feared someone might enter the room and see his failed attempt. The Virgin's mouth was sternly set—he couldn't think when he'd seen Elissa so grim. He carefully tore the canvas from the brads holding it to the slats and rolled it. He remembered there was a trash can on the street corner.

SOPHIE

"You're up pretty early, ain't ya, Perfessor?" Anna Anderson's figure, leaning on the broom she'd used to scrub the front sidewalk, blocked his path.

He was forced to hesitate. "Good morning, Mrs. Anderson. Yes, I suppose it is early."

"Best time of the day to get any work done, right?"

"Yes, indeed it is." He tried to move past her but she seemed reluctant to let him by without a further attempt at conversation.

"If you're thinking of wallpapering the house, you got to get permission, you know."

He looked at her uncomprehendingly, and she nodded toward the rolled canvas under his arm.

He flustered uncomfortably. "No, the apartment doesn't need it. This is just some student work I have to return."

"Oh, can I see?"

"No, if you don't mind—it's just a simple exercise. Now I must hurry. I have some shopping, some errands before class."

She held the door open for him. "Sure. Okay. It's not even seven-thirty, you know."

He forced his stoniest gaze. "As you yourself said, Mrs. Anderson, this is the best time of day to get any work done. Good morning."

He walked for half a mile before he found another covered trash basket on a corner where there appeared to be no one about. It was full, but he crammed the canvas in and moved some crushed paper cups and wrappers over it, then squared his shoulders as if proud of his accomplishment. He decided to take a walk before going to his cramped office at the University.

Better not go too far, though, he decided, as he felt the sharpness of the spring air penetrate his coat.

There seemed to be birds everywhere about him this morning, and their persistent chirping seemed to ease him from the personal preoccupations of the earlier hours. He took a less familiar street to avoid the morning traffic, which was just becoming more noticeable. A small park, half concrete, where a children's playground had recently been added, seemed to offer the calm he was searching for.

The painting was all wrong. He felt he'd somehow betrayed Elissa's memory and he began to berate himself. As if it weren't mostly vanity at the root of his discomfort, he thought. What if Dean Whitcomb did make him a little uneasy with his suggestions—and really, there was always a chance he did Whitcomb an injustice by supposing his intentions were guided by anything but a desire to be helpful.

How selfish he had been in the last few years. When there was Elissa by his side he had time to consider others far more. What had he really done to justify himself since then besides his job? Very little. There was that boy Louis, the first student he'd allowed himself to take an exceptional interest in for a long while. But wasn't that vanity too? The boy's talent was there before he chose to exert himself a bit on its behalf. Louis probably didn't need him as much as his own ego felt the need to associate with someone else's accomplishment.

The other students seemed somehow tiresome. The best of them, he reflected, would end up teaching in some backwater college or a dreary high school in the city. A few might move to other cities to be employed in advertising agencies, and most would eventually forget their earlier career goals to settle for a humdrum niche in the scheme of things. If nothing more exciting lay ahead for himself, he could envision even less for the hundreds who passed through his hands yearly.

Even Louis—did it really matter? His reflections didn't seem kind, and he chided himself mildly. He sat on a bench and lighted a fresh cigarette from his stub. The park was still empty, except for the birds who had already noticed the morning was no longer exclusively theirs and had begun to quiet down.

Of course, there was that pathetic Sophie Pappas, who probably worked harder than anyone in class. How unpleasant to think of her, and yet—her haunted eyes were ringed by circles that told him she was her family's slave, condemned to be a servant in return for their tolerating her education. She seemed to have fewer clothes than any girl in class, and the predominance of black in her wardrobe suggested the clothes were probably not of her own choosing, nor was she in all events likely to have been the first person to wear them. He wished she were more attractive. Sophie had sallow, pockmarked skin that had still not conquered its battle with acne, and there was an unpleasant display of gums when she smiled, which, he reflected, was happily not often.

He chided himself for his unflattering personal evaluation of her, but really, where could she hope to go? He had returned to a classroom one day last week and embarrassed her foraging through the wastepaper baskets for discarded tubes of paint that she might still squeeze enough pigment from to finish one of her projects. He had started to ask whether he might help her, but the shamed look on her face warned him off.

Of course she deserved a chance as much as most of those other dolts, who spent as much money on cosmetics or dates as they did on art supplies. He experienced a vague sense of guilt for not having recognized Sophie's problem sooner. She had about a year of school left toward her master's degree, he reflected. Such an intense creature! It would no doubt be awful if something were to prevent her from finishing. But perhaps with fewer worries she might prove as promising as most of the other candidates. She *needed* help; never mind whether she deserved it.

He fished through his breast pocket for one of his checkbooks. The account that he maintained exclusively for ordinary expenses had swollen to over $8,000 and all this was quite apart from investments long since planned by others toward the security of his ultimate retirement. He didn't even need to teach, and Sophie needed so much. He decided the only thing he could comfortably offer her was money, and that most discreetly. He'd have to go to the bank to cash a check. First he'd stop back at his apartment to address an envelope to her on his typewriter.

He had his students' names and addresses all neatly filed on three-by-five cards with comments made monthly on most of them. Best to take a couple of sheets of paper to wrap the cash in, and of course it would have to be sent by registered mail.

He felt very cheerful after making his decision and surprised Anna Anderson by smiling broadly at her when he passed her for the second time.

He was one of the first customers at the bank and was irritated when told he would have to see a bank officer before he could be allowed to withdraw $5,000. Cheyne sat solemnly at the man's desk, prepared to tell him to mind his own business if he should ask why he wanted the money. Instead, the man very politely asked him for further identification. A waste of time, he thought, since the teller knew him perfectly well and he'd never seen this man before. The check was swiftly initialed and returned to the teller's desk. It seemed to him that everyone was avoiding looking at him, as if he were someone who'd entered a room with his fly open.

He sealed the money in an envelope and went across the street to the post office to register it and send it off to

Miss Sophie Pappas. He had hesitated when typing out her name. It seemed so much more natural to call her "So-fi-a," but when he had done so in class she'd corrected him sharply.

Well, that's done. He smiled, feeling superior to the teller, the bank vice president, and the arrogant fat man who took his letter at the post office and complained because there was no return address on the envelope.

He was still in high spirits when he arrived on campus. Dean Whitcomb passed him on his way to the office and he found himself greeting him more cheerfully than he ever had before.

Whitcomb paused in the corridor, evidently pleased at his colleague's good humor. "Elliott," he said, "you're looking very well. By the way, may I tell Mrs. Whitcomb that we're expecting you this Friday?"

Cheyne looked bewildered.

"There was an invitation in your box last week," he said gently.

Cheyne hesitatingly felt the bulk of his breast pocket and realized he'd been so busy with his *Madonna and St. Anne* over the weekend that he hadn't opened his correspondence.

"Yes, of course. I would have called. Very kind. Seven, did you say?"

"No, Elliott, it's just tea. Faculty jargon for cocktails. Five to five-thirty will be fine."

"Oh, yes," he flushed. He was nonetheless rather pleased with himself for not cringingly refusing an invitation as he so often did. "Forgive me. I'm hopeless without my calendar in front of me. I look forward to it. I'll call Mrs. Whitcomb later today."

"No need. I'm glad you can make it. We miss seeing you about, you know. Do you some good to throw the bull around for an hour or two with the rest of us."

Cheyne entered his office, still in the finest mood he'd enjoyed in a long time, to organize his notes for his opening lecture. Well, why not? It would be a stupid cocktail party, but why not? His mind flashed to the Indian silk tie with all the violet in it that he hadn't worn for years. Why not indeed!

He walked briskly into class several minutes early. Sophie was at a desk in the front row hunched over a notebook.

"So*fia*," he said.

"Sophie, please."

"I'm sorry. It's just that I prefer Sofia. I hope you will someday, too."

Her eyes narrowed hostilely. "What do you want, Professor?"

"I was going to ask you whether you'd like to prepare an informal presentation of some of your work for me. I'd like to see what progress you've been making." He tried hard to sound pleasant, but his eyes had already fastened onto the galaxy of blackheads that covered her rather large nose.

Her body stiffened and the corner of her mouth started to quiver.

"Professor, I've been trying. It's not always easy for me. If you just give me a little more time. You'll see. I'll be able to catch up."

He turned crimson. "That's not what I meant. That is, I think your work is quite good enough. I just wanted—"

"What the hell do you know!" Her eyes were filling with tears. "I've got less than one more lousy year here, and now you—" She broke off into sobs.

"Sofia, please."

"Sophie, goddamn it. All right, I'll get my work together for you, but you're going to have to wait till next Monday. It'll mean my whole damn weekend, you—"

He noticed gratefully that a group of students had entered the room and he walked quietly to his desk. He thought he could hear his own voice droning on lifelessly from another room for the next hour.

He stumbled to the art library as soon as class ended. Even his office was no longer a sanctuary. There was always a student with a stupid problem or a stupid question who felt he could knock on the door any time he felt like it. He selected a large book on Northern Italian painting and chose a table with no one at it.

He needed to work. He had to try another painting. His overall concept was an interesting one, he was sure, but he needed to wipe out the dismal failure of this week's attempt. The acrylics were a mistake. He needed the life of oils. Perhaps with a good Japan dryer he wouldn't be held back so long. But the smell. He loathed working in oils in a house he had to live in. No matter. Spring was here and he would keep the windows open while he worked and the door to his bedroom closed.

He thumbed through the entire book, pausing only briefly at each illustration, and then started again more slowly. Landscapes were a more interesting exercise for the men who first executed them than they were for him, he decided.

The scenes of Venice and other cities were such miracles of precision that to tamper with their composition would be infamous. Court portraits in jewelled robes with all that attention to texture he found rather boring. It was the portraits of saints that captured him. The fiasco with the Giorgione only made him more anxious to justify himself.

He narrowed himself down to a Veronese of St. Catherine of Alexandria, a Tintoretto of St. Jerome, and a Carpaccio of St. Sebastian. There were slides of all three in the library and he pocketed them to take home for further consideration.

He could hardly wait that evening until he had projected them one after the other on the white wall of his studio and studied them in turn. St. Catherine he decided was too Boadicean. There was something businesslike and aggressive about the way she grasped her lance that he found unpleasant. St. Jerome he favored more, because he decided now that he preferred a more universal subject. Here was a saint who had attracted nearly all painters of religious subjects, but then so had St. Sebastian. He flashed the projector from one back to the other. Certainly neither of the saints was as high in the arcana as many others, yet their likenesses filled museums. Holy old age and holy youth. They were both irresistably attractive as subjects, but the mystical appeal of St. Jerome was certainly stronger. And his lion. That was important. As important as Catherine of Alexandria's horse.

Yes, the aged flesh with its challenging texture, the contemplative eyes that burned with conviction, the traditional skull by his side. That put him off a bit; he associated it with post-Renaissance Spanish painting—altogether unpleasant. Then he studied St. Jerome's nose more closely. Where had he seen a nose like that? Expressive, even vigorous—Sophie!

No. It would be Sebastian. One single figure to focus on. The barest landscape. A torn body that for every artist had been the ultimate expression of martyred youth. No, it was far more than that. Far more. St. Sebastian was the quintessential nude youth. Christ crucified was always ascetic. Even the Pietà—Adonis in Venus' arms, he reflected—was warm, but hardly sensuous in the way Sebastian invariably was. Other male martyrs were either grotesque or gory, as witness all the ghastly paintings of St. Bartholomew or St. Lawrence. The martyrdom of St. Agatha and a few others allowed for female nudity, albeit equally gory, but tradition had linked the nude *qua* nude to the exclusively classical. Strange that none of the classical subjects he could think of ever expressed the erotic male as satisfactorily as St. Sebastian. Was there something vaguely sadomasochistic about the representation? Well, certainly some artists must have sensed it, but for it to have been as popular a subject for all the years before the arrival during the Renaissance of the neoclassical fashion for nudes—no, it was clearly the only occasion for depicting a handsome naked youth at a time when the subject might have been considered scandalous. Louis

XIV had a St. Sebastian next to his bed, he recalled, but he couldn't remember whose.

Why else would this relatively obscure saint, whose claim to sainthood was known to so few, be such a popular subject if it were not the occasion for depicting the idealized beauty of a young man. The thought intrigued him, and he hung a canvas on the wall for his preparatory sketch.

Head tilted to the right, left foot slightly forward and right leg bent. Incredible how highly formalized the depiction had become. And the eyes always open, reflecting pain at times, but usually entranced with visions of his Saviour. Of course, he wasn't killed by the arrows, Cheyne recalled. There was a woman, St. Ida, who took him down and nursed his wounds. He met a swifter death later when recaptured by the Roman soldiers. This cruel game they had played with him, the torture with arrows, could easily have sped him to his Maker, but it didn't. If the arrows were not fatal, perhaps it was because the soldiers did not intend him to die but wanted the beautiful boy for their sadistic sport. These thoughts intrigued him as he became absorbed in his project. This modeling of the elevated right hip seemed wrong to him, and he erased it to begin again. Fantastic how some painters could express sensuality in even the most unlikely curves of the body!

It was after dawn when he stopped working. The canvas seemed already to be glowing with the energy he had poured into it. He showered hurriedly, dressed, and sank into his easy chair to study the figure before going on to his first class. When he looked away at last, he was already ten minutes late.

He was able to take a nap for two hours in his office between classes, mercifully undisturbed, and when his last period ended he found himself walking home at twice his normal pace. He closed the door behind him and sighed with pleasure at the sight of his St. Sebastian, tied to the post as if waiting for him to continue his labors to bring him to fuller realization. He hurriedly changed into work clothes and set at once to modeling the features and the body.

The next day the figure of Sebastian was almost finished. Cheyne decided to eliminate some tiny figures in the far landscape—soldiers running from their dreadful act. The angel in the upper foreground, bearing the martyr's palm, he decided to retain, but he changed the tone of the billowing cloak to allow Sebastian to dominate the canvas more strongly.

Two days later he felt the painting was almost ready for glazing. He stared at the figure for over an hour, feeling a voluptuous pleasure in following every line of Sebastian's form. The draped loins suddenly irritated him. Why did he need to observe the trite convention of masking the nude's genitals? He would far more likely have been naked at the time of his torture. Roman soldiers could hardly be expected to grant him the modest grace of a shame cloth. He approached the canvas hesitantly. The drape seemed more and more superfluous. There was a fold that followed the inguinal line very pleasantly and another fold in opposition to the pelvic line. A natural representation of his genitals could do as much. He dabbed some turpentine on a sponge and started blotting lightly.

In less than an hour the skin tones of the body had been restored and Cheyne was applying the first brush strokes to the delineation of the genitals. After a few minutes he realized he was obscuring them. Another absurd convention, he thought, and drew them in more boldly. He worked in a patch of pubic hair exactly two shades darker than the glowing blond curls on the saint's head. But the penis color was all wrong, he decided. Entirely too dark. What would be the tones for a Venetian blond? A few minutes later he had satisfied himself. The penis was of modest proportion, with a foreskin that covered the head fully and showed a more delicate pink in shadow at its tip. He sank back into his easy chair for further contemplation. A shaft of spring sunshine dazzled him into wakening much later, and he realized that even if he didn't shower he had missed his first class. He staggered dazedly towards his bedroom and realized he was soaking wet again. He showered in cold water to shock himself into alertness, but his body seemed half-anesthetized. Damn, and this afternoon he would have to go to Dean Whitcomb's party. He shook his head numbly. At least the painting's finished. It might do me some good to get away from it for a few hours. He went into the studio again and touched the surface of the canvas tentatively. It was already dry and the colors seemed fixed in perfect harmony. He turned away, unable to look at it more closely. He knew that all through the day, when he least expected it, the image of Sebastian would be flashing into his consciousness as clearly as the projection slides he showed.

I've been working too hard, he mumbled to himself. *Got to get away from it*. He chose a dark suit that he hardly ever wore, then returned to the closet to select a tie, and when he opened it he drew back quickly as if expecting to see someone inside. This wouldn't do. He fumbled through the rest of his dressing and left the apartment, taking great care not to let his eyes wander toward the canvas in the studio.

There was a package on the console table in the living room. Sophie had left it on his desk several days ago and it was still unopened. He picked it up as if judging its weight and dropped it again.

Anna Anderson was scrubbing the sidewalk when he passed her. She smiled briefly and returned to her work, shaking her head.

"The poor man ought to get some sun. All dressed up so nice and he still looks like he's been in a cellar for a year."

DEAN WHITCOMB

Dean and Mrs. Whitcomb entered the restaurant where they were meeting his unmarried sister for dinner. The only reasonable way to end a faculty tea at the hour you wished was by having a firm engagement for dinner, and Agnes was cooperative enough to telephone an hour before they wished guests to leave to confirm the engagement so the telephone conversation could be heard by all present. And there was no danger of feeling the need to urge anyone to join them. They had all met Agnes.

Agnes rose when they approached her table. "It must have been some party. You both look all in. Do you think it's wise to serve alcohol in this warm weather?"

Dorothy Whitcomb raised her arm wearily at her sister-in-law.

"I could still use one. A good stiff martini. You too, Barney?"

He nodded as he pushed his wife's chair in and signaled the waiter.

"And sherry for you, Agnes?"

"Yes, just a spoonful, thank you. Well, how did your tea go?"

"I may be able to tell you, but certainly not until I get another martini into me," moaned Dorothy.

"The usual people? Five faculty, three graduate students, and two friends?"

"Shut up, Agnes."

Barney Whitcomb squeezed his wife's hand. "A bit more trying than usual. One of our professors is getting a little ding-a-ling, and then we had another uninvited guest."

"Oh Barney, not now."

"No, I'd like to hear," chirruped Agnes. "Even if you think I'd be bored at these affairs, I still like to hear about them. Who was the uninvited guest?"

"Not a guest exactly. The mother of one of our students. A Greek woman. She could hardly speak English."

"But her screaming was matchless."

"I don't know why that stupid bitch in the office is so quick to offer my number when these things come up. The woman didn't even phone first."

"Of course she had reason to be distraught," said Dorothy. "Did I ever see this daughter of hers?"

"Sophie? No, I don't think so. And if you had I don't think you'd remember her."

"Why?" asked Agnes pertly.

"She was rather plain, not the sort one notices."

"Oh, I see," Agnes answered, looking around for the waiter with the drinks. "She must be very intelligent, though."

"No, not really. She squeaked through to graduate school but I don't think any of her professors finds her performance in any way remarkable."

"Well, what did her mother want?"

"To shake the heavens, more or less," Dorothy said. "Once she was at the front door there was nothing to do but let her in before the neighbors sent for the police."

"Totally irrational, but I suppose not unusual for these types. She holds the University responsible for everything that's happened to her daughter."

"Perhaps the only interesting thing that's ever happened to her."

"Well, for heaven's sake, what?" said Agnes, who had tossed off her sherry in one swallow.

"Sophie Pappas, as I say, is rather a simple girl. Her brothers had no college, and her family was still a little leery about her ambitions. As I understand it from that woman's rantings—you should have seen her, all black including the shawl, right out of *Zorba*. There's a traditional wail Greek women seem to have." He crooked his finger at the waiter for another round of drinks.

"I think I'll have one of those things you're having," said Agnes. "They look good."

"They're martinis," snapped Dorothy, "and you know damned well what happened last time you had one."

"Oh yes, martinis," said Agnes. "There was an article in *Viva* that said gin is more aphrodisiac for women than it is for men. Do you suppose that's true?"

"Be quiet, both of you. Three martinis, please. Anyway, as I was saying—the poor woman was actually raving. I think she was speaking English but I couldn't always be sure. When I was finally able to make sense of what she was telling me, and by now the whole tea was quite a disaster—"

"For heaven's sake, Barney, let me tell it if you can't get past Zorba and Greek wails! It seems a package with $5,000 cash in it arrived at the house for dreary little Miss Pappas. No return address, and apparently Sophia hadn't a clue, either. The family got hysterical, which seems to be effortless for them, and Mamma Pappas sent for a local midwife, probably one of those hideous women in black who do abortions with wire clothes hangers and had little Sophie checked out at once. She wasn't a virgin, of course. Who *could* be at her age!"

"I beg your pardon," Agnes hissed at her sister-in-law.

"All right, relax—I mean, unless of course they wanted to be. Does that make you feel better? Anyway, while the family was deciding whether to ship her off to a convent prison in Macedonia or whatever they do with their despoiled maidens, Sophie stole back the $5,000 and took off for Mexico City, apparently with a Puerto Rican beau who is not exactly white. They had a phone call from her this morning."

"And I, as dean of the department, am somehow held to be responsible for the little flower's fall. I believe Mrs. Pappas is convinced we have a course in what she called 'free love' in our curriculum."

"Poor woman. How did you get rid of her?"

"It was the oddest thing. I was about to call the police," Dorothy said, "when Professor Cheyne did the most beautiful job of upstaging her."

"Professor Cheyne? The widower?" Agnes had turned pink and perked up considerably. "He was at the last tea when I was still being invited to them. He was nice. Not a male chauvinist pig at all."

"Oh, for heaven's sake, cool it, Agnes. Yes, you met him. We even hoped—but never mind. The poor dear is getting stranger and stranger, and now it appears he's not at all well. Right toward the end of Mamma's jeremiade he passed out cold. And I do mean cold."

"It was quite alarming," said Barney. "I swear I couldn't find a pulse. He was already dead white when he came in, but that didn't surprise us since he's been odder than usual lately, as we were saying. The man's become rather a recluse. As a matter of fact, I was surprised he showed up. Anyway, when he had his attack I thought he had actually died, but then he started to move. His face was contorted by spasms of pain every minute or so, almost as if a knife were going in to him, and I swear it was the only sign of life I could find. It was a heart attack, of course. We sent for the meat wagon and they gave him some oxygen and tried to bring him to the hospital but he wouldn't hear of it. I must say his recovery was amazing. He even walked home."

"The poor man," Agnes clucked. "You should have asked him to dinner with us."

"I did. Actually I was afraid to have him even move, but the minute he started to come to he was very insistent on leaving at once. He kept muttering something about—Sebastian, I think. I assume he has a cat at home that needed to be fed. I'll call him later after dinner to see if he's all right."

BILL

The long days of summer often tempted Professor Cheyne to paint by the natural daylight at his open windows, but since he worked until he could no longer hold a brush, he resisted the urge, because he didn't trust the transition to artificial light. His control of the color key to all his paintings was the most important unifying element in them.

He scanned the living room walls, which were now almost completely covered by paintings, most of them framed. The style of the original artist was always evident, admirably so, but they were clearly all from Cheyne's brush.

He allowed himself the pleasure of surveying them all *en masse*, the only relief he took from his painting.

After the Carpaccio there had been a Guido Reni. How natural to move from his favorite Venetian atmosphere to the hotter, more florid attitude of the Neapolitans. The Reni St. Sebastian had an olive skin, heavy-lidded brown eyes only partly opened in their martyr's vision, and a ripe mouth; the lips almost objectionably full and red, he thought, but certainly faithful to the original. He had been given a coffee-colored penis with a rather longer foreskin than the Carpaccio, and heavy, pendulous testicles.

The Cranach next to it was more ascetic. Slanting

144

Flemish eyes with a finely chiseled brow line, and slender, almost girlish arms and legs. The narrow shoulders descended into the stylized roundness of abdomen and hips and Sebastian's penis was a small, smoothly curved arc surrounded by the faintest suggestion of almost colorless pubic hair. The figure seemed to be floating in an atmosphere so subtle and refined that the arrows could give no pain.

Rubens' St. Sebastian was fuller and florid, exhibiting the rounded muscles of a young warrior. The penis was exceptionally thick, and short enough to emerge almost horizontally, with the foreskin parted so as to reveal a bit of the red plum it enclosed.

Cheyne paused in his inspection and glanced at his watch. If he were to finish the Caravaggio this weekend he would have to go at once to the art supply shop. He had enough materials on hand to occupy him through the night, but it was Saturday, and he dared not risk being forced to stop his work because he'd run out of oil or turpentine.

He returned again to glance at the figure beginning to assume life on his canvas. The sensuous quality of Caravaggio's flesh tones was already evident. He stared harder and then pulled himself up abruptly. He mustn't allow himself to go off again, he thought. The periods he couldn't quite account for in the studio or the living room seemed to be occurring more frequently and he was taking longer to revive from them. When he went to class now he wore a rough rope around his waist, and the itching through the summer had been useful in distracting him from his reveries, but he wondered whether it would be as successful in the fall. He wondered what other measure he could adopt to keep that part of his consciousness alive that was necessary for him to continue his classes, which now were delivered largely by rote.

He checked his wallet carefully to be sure he had

enough money and started to leave, but when he got to the living room his eyes were riveted by the Füssli done during a very hot week in July.

"I should never have bothered with the decadents," he said half-aloud, but he remained riveted to the spot, focusing on the moonlighted flesh of an eerie Sebastian who looked almost carved from marble, the penis transformed by the cold light into a bloodless, sterile appendage. Cheyne snapped his head to rouse himself and fumbled for his door keys.

There was a car with a man sitting in it parked across the street from the house, and it seemed to Cheyne that he had noticed it there several times this week. He would have paid no attention except that the man stirred and looked self-conscious when Cheyne glanced at him.

Half an hour later when he returned from his shopping, the car was still there and Cheyne glanced at it a bit more curiously. The man inside was middle-aged, with very closely clipped gray hair. He opened the door and called out.

"Professor?"

Cheyne turned and blinked at him. "Yes?"

"I'd like a word with you, please."

"Have we met?"

"No, my name is Bill Miller. I'm a friend of one of your students."

Cheyne stared at him, less coldly than in bewilderment.

"Louis Denoyer."

"Yes?" Cheyne was now frowning.

"May we talk?"

"Of course, but I'm afraid you'll have to do the talking. I can't imagine—"

"Will you invite me inside, please? I won't be long."

"I'm afraid that's impossible."

"He is here, isn't he?"

"Denoyer? Of course not. Why would he be?"

"He hasn't been coming home evenings, and he says he's working on special projects for you."

"I have given him some special projects, yes, but he's certainly not expected to work on them in my home, and if he is working as assiduously as he says he is, I regret I can see no significant progress in the results. I suggest he has found some other occupation for his evenings that is more agreeable. We are a coed university, you know."

"He talks about you all the time. I thought—"

"Mr. Miller, I assume, though it is none of my affair, that you live with Louis?"

"Yes."

"I must tell you, then, that I prefer that it continue to be none of my affair. I'm afraid I can't help you."

"You won't speak with me?"

"About what, for heaven's sake? I regret—" He stopped and looked into Bill's face for a second. "No, I'm afraid—just go away, won't you please."

"Professor, I beg you." He reached out a hand and put it on Cheyne's sleeve and Cheyne drew away from him, shrinking as he now invariably did from any physical contact.

"Stop!" His voice rose sharply and then he noticed two policemen coming toward them and remained silent, hesitating to turn away. One of them, a tall, beefy blond, greeted the Professor solemnly by name and Cheyne mechanically nodded his head.

Bill started his motor quickly and drove off without saying goodbye. The professor stared at the young policeman who was still looking at him, seeming friendly but not smiling.

"Nicest time of the year, isn't it, Professor Cheyne?"

Cheyne continued to stare at him.

"Norman Ashe. I was in your class last year."

Cheyne nodded and mumbled something he hoped would be received as acceptable trivia, then turned and entered the house.

He was shaking when he put down his purchases. Stupid to have put on a necktie just to go for a few minutes shopping, he thought. He undressed completely and went into the studio to resume work on the Caravaggio. His eyesight seemed blurred when he looked around the room, but he was instantly able to focus clearly on his work. The hand that trembled when he reached for his brush became composed and sure as soon as it reached the canvas.

Relentlessly he began to remodel the genitals of the figure. It took him much longer than it did to add the final tones and highlights to the rest of the portrait. The brush was put down only when he was certain that he had completed his work.

The body of St. Sebastian seemed to be writhing sensuously, almost rubbing like a cat against the stake to which it was tied. The flesh glowed with pulsating life and the left leg was thrust sharply forward, pushing the penis into bolder relief, a thick corded slab of pink and mauve flesh that lay almost as if it were waiting to surge in response to unseen stimuli that surrounded it.

Cheyne fell to his knees and remained there until he lost consciousness. When he awoke it was a bright Monday morning, and he hurried to the bath to prepare himself for class, knowing without consulting his watch that it was time for him to be gone.

SODOMA

A week later Professor Cheyne was still agitated as he walked home from class. The impudence of that boy Louis! Did he think I couldn't see what he was doing, stretching his leg and flexing that way and rubbing his cock. What the hell does he think my classroom is, and exactly what is he trying to do with me!

The thought that Louis might be trying to seduce him never seriously occurred to Cheyne. The boy was simply obscene and ill-mannered.

"Sometimes I thank God I never had children," he muttered half-aloud. "If that were my boy—!"

He recognized a few yards ahead the policeman who had been a student of his. Oh Lord, he looks like he wants to be chatty. Cheyne stepped up his pace so he could pass by with the air of a man who is in an obvious hurry and should not be detained. The policeman sensed it and let him by with a cursory nod. Cheyne sighed and slowed his pace until he reached home.

He undressed quickly and directly himself to the work at hand. He knew the Sodoma would be a problem when he first saw the slide, and he had resisted it until he had exhausted all the other available Sebastians.

The archer in the foreground was almost as important to the composition as the body of Sebastian himself, and Cheyne habitually preferred to reduce the elements in the composition to the fewest possible. He had painted in the archer until such time as he could decide whether he must be kept or not.

By altering the plane encompassed by the original painting, he was able to emphasize Sebastian's figure so that if it should remain alone it would be able to dominate the landscape, but the archer still could not be ignored. The archer's back was to the viewer, well in the foreground and cut off just a few inches below the rounded buttocks that had been covered by a gauzy skirt, now eliminated. The archer's arms were held slightly apart from the body as he looked at Sebastian, suggesting awe of or even fascination with the martyr before him. He appeared to be a youth of the same age as Sebastian, but he had a more muscular, more mature body. The shoulders were broad and heavy and the high buttocks were full but hard, cutting in softly to the columnar thighs that stood sharply apart and then vanished into the border of the canvas.

Sebastian's eyes roved upward in a face that reflected at once the sweet spiritual bliss of his martyrdom and its pain. His blond curls hung damply on his shoulders and his lips were parted in a last prayer.

Cheyne stared at the painting for a while before he decided how he would finish it. The archer's importance had to be minimized. St. Sebastian's beauty, far greater than that reflected in any other canvas, had to dominate the painting more completely.

Cheyne set to work and in half an hour stepped back to consider his emendation critically. Sebastian now had a full erection, throbbing gloriously as in a final triumph over death, and the archer seemed to be—could he be?—yes, he was worshiping it. Cheyne instantly fell to the floor and lapsed into the void that would hold him till morning.

He dressed very carefully and at the last moment decided to leave off his customary necktie. It had taken all his conscious effort this last week to keep from fainting in class, and although his legs felt strong and his head seemed clearer he knew that at any moment the beginnings of that soft wave that transported him could approach—and would have to be fought off. He felt inside his shirt for the carefully concealed pins to be sure they were neatly in place. A little pressure when he felt the wave coming on, and, unseen by his class, he could produce enough pain to bring his senses into focus. There was never more than an occasional drop of blood and these stains he washed out easily before sending his shirts to the laundry. He stood in front of the bathroom mirror for a moment and the lightness began to overtake him. So soon. No, the pins would not be enough.

He went to his dresser and found a pair of garters he had not worn in years and took one of them into his studio. He doubled the garter and studded it with thumb tacks, then dropped his trousers and stretched the garter around his genitals. There were a dozen tiny points of steel cutting into him, but not very painfully. He tried pressing his thighs together, and his eyes blurred with tears at once. He tried sitting and crossed his legs and there was an even stronger reaction to the pain. He checked himself to see whether his actions had produced any blood. There were tiny purple dots studding his penis and testicles, but the pin points had not entered deeply enough to draw blood. Satisfied, he readjusted the elastic and drew his trousers back on, then studied himself in the mirror. His crotch was neat and gave no indication of the device it held.

As he walked into his first class he felt comforted by the tiny jabs that every step produced. The class seemed inattentive and vague that day, and he was grateful for the chance to give his lesson without too many questions or other interruptions. His eyes passed from one blank face to another until he reached the back of the room where Louis was sitting. How could he dare? Louis was wearing a blue-and-white striped T-shirt molded neatly to his chest and the same white jeans he had worn a few days ago. He had arrogantly stretched his left leg down the aisle again and his penis was neatly outlined in the tight, white jeans. Cheyne gritted his teeth. Girls without bras and boys showing themselves off flamboyantly in too-tight trousers! He was used to that; there was scarcely a class in which an instructor might not easily be distracted by a careless or discretely planned display of sex. Louis' presumption was unmistakeable. Cheyne watched his hand fall casually along the length of his penis and then gently begin to move across the shaft.

Cheyne jerked his thighs together and the pain cut into him sharply, making him gasp for a moment in the middle of a sentence. The class appeared not to notice. Cheyne's lapses had become so frequent they were accepted as a normal part of his delivery. He paused a moment. Louis' penis had unmistakeably begun to harden and there was an arrogant smirk on the boy's mouth. Cheyne pressed his thighs together again, less sharply, and looked at his watch. The class was only little more than half over. He tried to avoid looking at the boy but his gaze would wander back uncontrollably, still indignant at his boldness and too angry to be anything but indifferent to whatever charms the boy thought he displayed.

Exactly what did he think he was doing! Cheyne glared angrily at him, but Louis arched his back and laced his hands behind his neck while he pretended a long, luxurious yawn that allowed him to thrust into full view the penis that was now turgid and fighting against the restraining fabric of his trousers. Cheyne crossed his legs and pressed slowly until he felt his anger pass.

When the class ended, Cheyne waited quietly at his desk. He knew Louis would come to speak to him when the rest of the students had gone. He struggled to compose himself and formed exactly the words he would say to the boy. He was now there and had the supreme arrogance to stand pressed against his desk, as if his intended message was not yet entirely clear.

Cheyne cleared his throat. "I don't like your games. They're cheap." He was going to add, "And they don't interest me," but he felt that should already be sufficiently clear.

If Louis felt rebuffed he gave no sign. His lips curled in a smile of mock innocence. "Why, Professor, I don't understand. If I were to play games with you, I don't think they'd be cheap."

Cheyne crossed his legs and pressed until he almost cried out with the pain, then drew his hand back and struck the boy a stinging blow across the mouth. He looked with horror at the imprint of his hand across the face and the drop of blood that appeared at the lips, then felt a warm trickle running down his thighs. He would have to hurry to the faculty lounge to dry himself before his trousers showed a dark stain.

He shook his head to clear it. "Don't forget to bring me your work tomorrow."

He left the room quickly before Louis could show any recovery from the shock of the blow.

Cheyne inspected himself hurriedly in one of the toilets of the faculty lounge, hoping no one would enter, despite the privacy of the locked booth.

There were crusts of blood clotting the hair along his groin and he had to wipe the still-fresh blood off with paper. He would have to go home at once. No, he dare not try another class. He threw the garter into the bowl and was relieved when it flushed away at the first attempt.

He had work to do. He thought of the finished Sodoma, which he would now transfer into its waiting frame and then hang in the most prominent spot in the living room. He thought of it reverently—his finest accomplishment, and a work clearly superior to that of the master whose hand had first dictated it. Now he was ready for the final test. All available slides of other painters' Sebastians were exhausted, and his living room could accommodate only one more. It would be his own.

The final tribute. A Sebastian that would be an amalgam of every artist's attempt to bring life to the beautiful martyr. He inspected the front of his trousers carefully. There were a few dark traces but they would certainly escape notice. After all, he wasn't wearing tight white trousers like that disgusting boy. That filthy pervert!

SEBASTIAN

Cheyne finished stretching the canvas across the wooden frame and felt the taut smoothness of the surface. It had been a struggle to get it perfectly stretched, even though the frame was built with supporting struts to keep it rigid and square. He had never worked on a canvas this large before, but he wanted the figure of Sebastian to be fully life-sized.

The canvas measured two meters wide and three high, classic proportions, and he noted with satisfaction that it would need a wall entirely of its own to be viewed properly. He moved a ladder into place and started a quick charcoal sketch of the essential features of his composition. It would be only a matter of transferring to the canvas the elements that were already clearly delineated in his imagination. There was not a tree on the horizon whose position he was not certain of, not a nuance of the saint's posture that wasn't already perfectly determined.

He worked through the night and then moved his easy chair into the studio so that he might gaze at the work in progress while he rested. The portrait clarified as soon as he sank into the chair, and the oblivion that he knew would overtake him descended at once while the image of St. Sebastian burned itself into his brain.

When he awoke there was no thought of going to class. It did not occur to him to phone the office to say he was ill and couldn't come in for a few days. By now the work at hand had absorbed him so completely that he was no longer even conscious of the need to eat or to relieve himself. His image of Sebastian was as clearly imposed on the canvas as if a slide projector had flashed it there and he needed only to add pigment to the surface to give it a firmer dimension.

It must be done as quickly as possible. Now he didn't dare allow himself to slip into his easy chair even for a moment. The canvas dictated sternly what he must do, and he followed its direction ecstatically.

Another day passed and his hand seemed to move more slowly, as if forcing itself through a medium denser than air as he added the final tones. When it was finished he no longer needed to look at it to be certain that every last detail was in place. The canvas glowed as if a strong light had been placed behind it. Space receded and advanced from every angle of vision, and the saint's body seemed more sculpted than painted, so clearly did it emerge in every curve and plane.

He moved back from the painting and groped for his chair, ready now for the oblivion it offered.

The skin across the back of his hands prickled and he was aware that he was not alone.

He turned his head slowly toward the door to the living room and saw him standing there, dressed in a blue-and-white striped T-shirt and white jeans.

"Sebastian," he murmured.

The figure advanced until it stood directly in front of him, blocking his view of the canvas and yet almost exactly replacing the figure on it.

"Sebastian, forgive me."

The figure slowly removed the T-shirt and jeans and stood before him naked.

"I'm sorry I offended you. I didn't know. It was your beauty."

"My beauty!" he sneered. "Are these beautiful?" He pointed to the deep gashes that laced the length of his body in a savage network. "Answer me. Are these beautiful?"

"Yes. I think they are."

"Then think of them again. Did you ever feel my *pain*? Do you think that figure lashed to the post was something that you should admire for the curve of its leg, the arch of its neck, the sweet expression of its mouth? Did you once think of what I suffered, of what I sacrificed to my God?"

"Yes, I did, I did."

"Artists! You admired the beauty of the landscape, the skilled way a crafty hand created a new perspective or a foreshortening, the happy addition of a few birds warbling over my head or the discreet handling of color. Could you feel the arrows entering, the humiliation of standing naked before my tormentors, my bloody sacrifice?"

"Forgive me, Sebastian, forgive me."

"Then think, now, of the real beauty of these wounds."

He approached Cheyne where he had sunk to his knees and drew closer. Cheyne saw the chest before him with a raw gash that had torn into the flesh just a few inches in front of his mouth and he leaned forward to kiss it.

"Sebastian," he murmured. His mouth explored the rent flesh and his tongue felt the tip of a broken rib jutting sharply inside it. He sucked it and felt the warm blood fill his mouth.

"Sebastian," he whispered again, and his mouth moved from wound to wound, kissing them and sucking the blood from them. He looked up at the martyr's face and the eyes were sparkling like fiery stars. He embraced the body and sought to kiss him on the mouth.

The breath from his nostrils had an incredible sweetness and the walls of the room seemed to shimmer and move off into an infinite distance.

An ecstasy beyond any he had dreamed swept into him and his arms encircled the body tightly, more tightly, until he felt himself dissolve into it and he was released.